Murder Manatee

Ben Theo Pelagic

Edited by www.abbywoodland.com

This book is dedicated to all of my friends and family. They reminded me time and time again of who I am, and what I am capable of. Without their love and support this book would have never been written.

I would also like to take a moment to recognize all those who have been lost, at sea or otherwise. You are not forgotten. To all those who feel lost. I wish that you will be found. Sometimes when you are lost you need to find something for yourself.
Stay strong and never give up.

To the reader: Thank you for taking the time to read this book and my humble dedication. Without you my work is severely lacking. I write these stories not just because I love them dearly. It is also because I want to bring joy and entertainment to as many people as I can. My stories are not for everyone. That is something I have to accept. All of my stories are written to my satisfaction. You will never see my name on a book I am not proud of. I work tirelessly to ensure the quality of your experience. That being said, I am not perfect and I do make mistakes. If there is something you do not like or think was done in error please let me know. I enjoy criticism far more than praise. With critique I can improve, with praise I stay the same. If you feel so inclined I would love to hear from you.

Contents

Introduction: Author's Note

This next portion does not pertain to the story. If you have cave diving experience you are probably familiar with the story of Debra Eaves. I believe it is important context and history that deserves to be remembered. You will not miss any of the story if you skip this section. However, I strongly encourage you to stick around for this part.

Cave diving is a very dangerous and risky hobby. Cave divers go through rigorous training and utilize advanced skills and special equipment to mitigate that risk.

In 1989, Debra was diving with her boyfriend when she experienced an issue with her primary dive light. While Debra and her boyfriend resolved the issue, they had floated away from the dive line in the cave. When they relocated the dive line, they traveled along for some time. Once her boyfriend had noticed he didn't recognize the features in this section of the cave, he got Debra's attention. He tried to explain that they were going the wrong way.

Unfortunately, Debra did not believe him. She unknowingly continued deeper into the cave. Her boyfriend turned around and exited the cave. What he must have gone through is unimaginable. This was in the age before cellphones. When he exited the water, he drove to the dive shop not far from the springs. He believed getting help was the best course of action.

When help arrived, they found Debra's body not far from where they had their disagreement. Debra's unwitting sacrifice was an entirely avoidable tragedy. Because of this, a new standard was created. It was agreed that a permanent, larger, more resilient, and color coded line would be placed as the main line that would lead toward the exit. This would give divers visual and tactile differences they could use to distinguish the line leading out of the cave.

After explaining the purpose the line would be used for, a distributor sold the line at cost. Gold line was what they just happened to have a surplus of at that moment. Soon after, caves around the country would replace thousands of feet of line. Now caves around the world can be found with gold main line.

While it is impossible to know how many fatalities have been prevented since the implementation of gold line, it has undoubtedly saved lives. It has forever changed cave diving. Every day cave divers are able to find their way back to the surface safely and confidently because of Debra's unwitting sacrifice.

This story isn't widely known outside of the cave diving community. Not all divers know this story, and even fewer non-divers are aware of it.

During my research for this book it seemed impossible to find Debra's name published anywhere. While I understand and respect people's decisions to protect privacy, this was a historical and important event.

Debra deserves to be remembered, not cast aside, and certainly not forgotten. Please remember and share her story.

I would like to add a quick reminder to all divers. Your death is avoidable. Never dive beyond your skill level. Always make sure you have the appropriate training for the dive you are planning. Stay in shape and take care of your body. Always make sure you have the appropriate gear. Never dive unless you are feeling 100%. It's just not worth the risk. Stay safe out there.

Thank you for reading this additional section of true diving history.

Preface

For hundreds of years, men have traversed the rivers of the United States of America. For equally as long, men have told stories of the monsters that dwell within.

In 1822, the Tennessee River was host to tales of a giant serpent. During July 1916, the residents of New Jersey would be savagely attacked by what was believed to be a large shark that had gotten lost from the sea. During the era of World War Two, the people of Pennsylvania and West Virginia would be terrorized by a monster that lived in the Monongahela River. In 1971 a giant animal with a spiny dorsal fin and grey skin would kick off a media frenzy in Arkansas. All of these are real world legends. They involved real people, and sadly some of those people lost their lives. Some of these river beasts live in massive raging rivers like that of the Mississippi. Others are reported in tiny streams.

As recently as 2026, a juvenile great white named "Contender" entered the tidal water ways of Indian River Florida. Bull sharks have been recorded traveling as far as Alton, Illinois in the Mississippi.

The story you are about to read is fiction, however one fact remains...even freshwater rivers are not free of large predators.

I would like to shift focus slightly.

Now let's talk about remote operated vehicles. "ROV" is a term used primarily to describe submersible watercraft that do not carry passengers. As you will read in the story, there are many classes of ROV. If you felt so inclined you could watch a video online and after a modest investment build your own. Exploring under water with what amounts to an underwater drone is very fun. In most cases it is also cheaper than getting the gear and certification to SCUBA dive. It is also infinitly safer. A quality, ready-built ROV at the time of writing costs as little as $600. I personally have a model that would have cost $2,000.

Fortunately, through my work, I was able to get it for free. They are immensely fun and surprisingly intuitive to operate. However, commercial grade ROVs cost significantly more—roughly $12,000 with the necessary equipment to exceed the capabilities of cheaper models. Though the kind used for actual commercial work like research expeditions, or oil rig inspections often cost in excess of forty-thousand-dollars. The ROV described in this story would be comparable to a model with a nearly twenty-thousand-dollar price tag.

Let's talk about cave diving. This is one of, if not the deadliest, hobbies in the world. It requires extensive training and knowledge to be done safely. That being said, with the correct training and equipment it is no more dangerous than driving to work in the morning. If you are interested in reading more about the topic I cannot recommend anyone more highly than Rob Neto. His books are fantastic and go into much deeper depth of detail than my books do. What is covered in this book just barely scratches the surface. I am not a scuba diver let alone a cave diver. (However I plan on changing the former this year.) Therefore, I do not feel qualified to go into much detail on the topic. I will however say that I have researched the topic extensively.

What I will tell you is this—you have not experienced true panic until you have a problem underwater and cannot simply take a breath of fresh air to calm down. Now imagine that level of panic but it is physically impossible to ascend straight to the surface. Think about that for a moment. What do we do when we are stressed? We breathe faster. What do we do when we need to calm down? We take a deep breath. We, as mammals, require air to breathe. It is deeply coded within us that *air is life* and without it, we will die. Words cannot describe the primal terror of needing to breathe. Of having your body screaming at your brain to take a breath and not being able to do so.

Chapter One

Cody

The Heat was getting to him. Sweat dripped down his nose, and he was worried it would drip onto the circuit board in front of him. He couldn't wipe it away though. He needed to focus. He held the wires in both hands. He had tined them with solder already, the soldering iron still clamped in his teeth as he leaned into the boat.

Next time, he would take the part out and solder it at his bench. This was a pain in the ass. He was really worried about dropping the soldering iron between his legs. That would be horrific. Castrated by a soldering iron. A worse fate was hard to imagine.

The tip of the iron heated the wire, and the two blobs of solder on the tined wires became one. He pulled his head back and waited a second before tugging the wires. It was a good connection. He slid the heat shrink over the new splice and held his lighter close enough to make it shrink over the wires. Now he just needed to pull the soldering Iron out of his mouth and place it in the coiled stand balanced on the center console.

He grabbed it and immediately knew something wasn't right. He had let go with his teeth by the time he realized what had happened. He was holding the hot end between his fingers. He thought about the alternative if he dropped it. That would hurt a lot worse. He grabbed the handle with his teeth again, and looked at his fingers. The skin was bright yellow and looked like it was coated in a powder.

That couldn't be good.

He picked up the coiled stand and brought it to his mouth instead. Then he set the malicious contraption down and rushed into the house. He ran to the sink and let the water run for a moment. With his left hand he checked the water temperature to make sure it wasn't too cold and definitely not hot. Satisfied with the temperature, he thrust his hand into the water. It felt good. He had never burnt himself this bad before. He felt like an idiot. He wondered how long it would take to heal. It stung but didn't really hurt as much as he thought it would when he saw it. His aunt stormed into the kitchen from her office.

"Cody! What happened?"

"I uh, decided since I had never grabbed the hot end of my soldering iron before I'd give it a shot. It was not great."

"Do you need to go to the hospital?" she asked.

"I don't think so. It wasn't dirty. All they are going to do is clean it, put ointment on it and bandage it up. I can do that here."

"If your fingers fall off, it's your fault."

"I know," Cody replied.

He pulled his hand from the water and looked at it. His thumb and index finger were fine, about as bad as grabbing a hot pan from the oven. The back of his middle finger was cauterized. With his injury treated, he walked back out into the blazing sun and looked at his boat. He was proud of his handy work. He still had to close it all up, but it was finally done. Three months of research, trial and error, and dozens of 3D print iterations from his friend Brian's printer meant he was now the proud owner of an underwater ROV.

Short for a Remote Operated Vehicle, ROV's were used to view things underwater without putting anyone at risk. They were often used for locating problems with underwater equipment before a dive team risked their lives to make the repairs. They were also very popular for research.

Cody loved the water, and he dreamed of being able to SCUBA dive. His chronic asthma had other plans though. He tried a couple of times, but he struggled to clear his mask of water, and complete other skills necessary to become certified. An ROV, basically an underwater drone, was the closest he would get. ROV's could cost tens of thousands if not hundreds of thousands of dollars. There were some cheaper alternatives that did work but they had their limits and for half the price he could build it himself. It would end up costing him seven thousand dollars, almost four times the cost of the intermediate ROV he had considered buying previously.

His, however, had a working depth of over a thousand feet and could deploy twice as much cable. He could collect items in an onboard storage container since it had two fully articulated mechanical arms, and 5 cameras. One of those cameras accounted for two thousand dollars of the project. The other majority of the cost was in the two thousand feet of tether cable that had to be connected to the ROV.

ROV's, unlike drones, must be connected by a cable or tether to the operator in order to be controlled. Radio waves and infrared do not travel underwater. So, WiFi and Bluetooth do not work. There are some interesting developments in using sound based wireless information transmission, however this is for transmitting data and it is very slow. It has yet to be utilized for controlling underwater equipment. So instead, a cable is required, and managing that cable is extremely difficult.

The ROV Cody thought about buying had a manually operated spool. Which meant he would have to unwind and reel in the cable manually, on top of having to pilot the ROV.

That settled it.

He would build his own.

He felt really stupid a couple weeks ago while looking for parts on a dodgy Chinese factory direct seller website. He saw almost exactly the same ROV he was building. He showed his friends Brian and Mark one night while they were hanging out. They got a good laugh out of it. It did everything their drone did, that was true.

"Yeah, but ours has a much better camera and a way better user interface I bet. Look at how they're achieving trim. Those are manual weight slots. Ours has multiple ballast tanks. That one has a wireless-only connection to the remote. Ours connects directly to a computer and we can stream the dives live, or watch them on a full size monitor. Look! It says rechargeable. Dude, they can only dive for three hours. Ours is directly powered by the boat. We can dive indefinitely. Ours is better. Besides, ours is still cheaper right?" Brian stated.

It wasn't.

The Chinesium doppelganger was about two thousand dollars cheaper. Brian had a good point though. Theirs was indeed better. That was then, this was here and now, Cody was excited. He closed everything up. He paid out the cable from the spool and set the ROV on the cart he used for yard work, then wheeled it back to his aunt's pool. He splashed the ROV and jumped in with it. He spun it and tilted it, held it upside down, then walked it around the pool. The gyroscope was now calibrated.

He hopped back up on the boat, and typed on the keyboard of the control and monitor box mounted to the center console—WASD to move around, Q to ascend, and E to descend. Z made it rotate left, while X rotated it right. The ROV was working, and the spool was paying out cable, laying back on the spool in neat perfect rows when it retracted.

He pulled out his phone and took a video. He sent it to Brian and Mark. He also sent it to his fishing buddy, Jose. Cody invited them to go with him to do a real-life field test. He had already done a depth test for the capsule that held the electronics before the ROV was assembled, but he was still a little nervous about testing it all together. He was much more excited about what he might see though.

After cleaning up and taking a well-deserved shower, Cody's phone rang. It was work. There was an emergency four hundred miles away. It would be a week-long project assuming things went well. He couldn't say no, even if he wanted to. He was on call, and he also needed the money to recover from the financial burden of building the ROV. He wondered if this would open any doors for him, and if he could make a living with his new creation.

He probably could.

The work trip went well. Really well. Cody made an extra three grand from the scrap left over from the demo alone. When he arrived back in town he deposited his small fortune before heading home to his aunt's house.

When he walked in, the smell of beef stroganoff slapped him in the face. She knew he was coming home today and was preparing one of his favorite meals.

Cody started living with his aunt after his divorce was finalized. His goal was to get away from the bad influences and put a stop to his drinking. His ex-wife hated his drinking. She said Cody's drinking is what drove her into another man's arms. He knew his drinking was a problem, but his bills were paid. He had never had a DUI either, well not officially anyway. He was a high functioning alcoholic. Some would consider him a savant, others would say he was an arrogant prick. His divorce was a fall from grace.

When he was married, he was on top of the world, and he felt as if he had everything.

After he lost his house and realized his wife was cheating on him, he started looking inward. He had never really thought of himself as having flaws or needing work. Sure he could be better, there were always new things to learn or skills to refine, he just didn't believe he had any negative traits. He started looking at his friends too, or at least the people he called friends. When he needed a place to stay everyone had an excuse.

That's when he realized his employer had work in Florida. He had stayed down there before in a hotel to help the Florida team catch up when they got overwhelmed. He liked the panhandle, especially Fort Walton Beach where his aunt lived. It was far enough away that he could try for a fresh start of sorts. He still missed it back at home though. He missed the road-runners, the sunsets, and the beautiful night sky he grew up beneath. Florida was too bright at night and you couldn't really see the stars. Not like in Arizona. He chuckled at the thought that it would be colder in Florida. Most people would not consider Florida to be colder than their home state. Cody told his aunt about the job and thanked her profusely for the amazing food. Not to mention all the support she had given him over the past year and a half.

"It's nothing sweetie. That's what you do for your family. Besides, it isn't a one sided arrangement at all. It's nice having someone around since your uncle passed. Your cousins hardly ever visit from back home. You have been a big help around the house too."

"Thanks, Mimi. I don't know where I'd be without you."

After dinner Cody went to the Kava bar down the road to meet with Brian and Mark. He thundered down the road in his big red truck listening to the radio and singing along. When he pulled in, he saw Mark's motorcycle and Brian's car parked in their usual spots. He busted in the door and the kava tender, Eddy, greeted him loudly.

"AY! Cody! Where ya' been? Started thinking you might be dead."

"-SEISMIC ACTIVITY IN NORTH FLORIDA HAS EXPERTS CONCERNED AS-"

The TV above the bar was loud and hard to hear over.

"I had a last minute work trip in Ft. Myers. They put me up in a hotel. You know how that goes. Perdiem, hotel reward points, scale pay, and the scrap metal was insane. I couldn't turn it down. Speaking of turning things down, can you lower the volume on that thing?"

"Yeah, got you," Eddy responded.

"Cody, did you get the thing I sent you? I found a possible solution to the video transmission," Brian said as he gave Cody a fist bump.

"Yeah, I did. I like it. What's good Mark?"

"Fucking still can't get on a good sleep schedule. That shit with my Mom's got me all fucked."

"Damn, still?"

"Yep, I woke up twenty minutes ago. I didn't go to sleep until ten AM."

"Shit. What about you Brian? Anything new?"

"Just basic work stuff. We had a vendor meet up yesterday. They brought us some food and showed us some new products. It was fun. We are still playing catch up since the shipping issue in the Panama Canal."

"Right on. So, what are you guys doing tomorrow? You down for the first official field test? I'm pretty sure Jose is coming too."

"Fuck yeah! Count on it dude," Mark said excitedly.

"Me too, I've got nothing going on tomorrow. We going out off Adam's Point?"

"Nah, I want to hit Buffalo Breakdown."

"C'mon man. First trip out and you don't want to take it in the ocean?" Mark asked.

"Not really. It just doesn't seem as interesting to me," Cody replied, shrugging.

"Dude, the ocean is way cooler. Don't you like sharks? Bikini babes? Brian back me up on this."

"Not gonna lie, the ocean does sound cooler than the river." Brian joined in on Mark's side.

"No way! What about the caves? What about the sunken treasure down there? Besides, I don't want it in the salt until we are one hundred percent sure everything is water tight. Plus, visibility will be way better and the water will be way more calm."

"If you say so I guess. I'm going no matter what," Mark agreed begrudgingly.

"Ditto. Count me in," Brian added.

"Sweet, meet up at the boat ramp at seven."

"Shit, I need to get home and try to get some sleep then. Hey, Eddy! Can I cash out?"

"I got you," Eddy called out as he grabbed the handheld and walked over.

Mark went home, so Cody, Brian, and Eddy talked for a while, catching up. They discussed the ROV and the various things they were excited and worried about. In order to be up on time, they called it a night relatively early for a Friday at ten-thirty. The drive home was longer than usual that night. Cody felt an immense pressure building in his chest. The possibility of failure lingered in his mind.

His home wasn't any further away. But it felt like it was taking forever. Each red light felt like an eternity. It wasn't until he was at the stop sign just before his neighborhood that he realized he hadn't had any music or podcast playing in the background. His thoughts had been roaring in his mind. All of his hard work had come to this moment. He could succeed or he could fail. The thought of failure chipped away at his composure. By the time he stumbled into the house, he was on the verge of tears. There was so much pressure all of the sudden. The anxiety was crushing. He turned on the kitchen sink and splashed cold water on his face. Then he felt his aunt place her hand on his shoulder.

"What's the matter?"

"I don't know. Everything just felt like it was falling over on top of me. It just came out of nowhere. I feel like if I fail I'll be letting everybody down."

"Sweetie, you have nothing to be worried about. Your friends won't care if something goes wrong. Not to mention it wouldn't be the first time something went wrong. It would be just another problem for you boys to solve together. Honestly I don't think anything is going to go wrong. With how hard you have been working on that thing, I don't think you would be willing to take it out unless you believed it was ready."

"Thank you Mimi, you're the best aunt ever. I really needed to hear that. I feel a lot better," Cody said as he hugged his aunt.

The morning was slow to arrive. Cody hitched the boat and made sure they would have everything they needed, then he drove down the road towards the boat ramp. The gurgling thumping motor of his truck came to a halt in the parking lot of the gas station where he stopped before arriving. Cody didn't need gas but he did want an egg and cheese croissant and a cup of coffee. He grabbed aside of hashbrowns too, then he was back on the road. The vintage punk rock he was fond of rang in his ears as the wind crashed into his face. Cody was glad he didn't smoke anymore. It was expensive and he was glad his lungs were strong and could appreciate the morning air.

The first edge of sunlight peeked over the horizon as Cody tied off the boat. Brian's car burbled as the turbo purged through its blow-off valve. He down shifted with a crackling racket as he rolled into the parking lot, gravel crunching under the tires. Jose had beaten them both there and was already helping guide the boat off the trailer. Mark, as usual, was nowhere in sight.

They loaded up into the boat. Brian exhaled a cloud of nicotine vapor and the sound of Mark's bike resonated through the air. Mark cracked the throttle a couple times as he pulled into a parking spot. He also lit up a cigarette as he walked down the boat ramp. The boat lurched as he climbed aboard, and as it settled, the sound of water lapping at the hull filled their ears.

They went over their plan. They would motor down the Hom-puks-chee-hatchee River until they got to Buffalo Breakdown. The breakdown was a large sinkhole in the middle of the river. It was half a mile wide and four hundred feet deep. It acted like a small lake allowing for very little current and in exchange very calm water. It opened up to multiple caves as well. It would be the perfect place to really test out the ROV at depth and see how well it would maneuver.

They were all excited to see what was down in the sink hole. It seemed like everyone knew somebody that knew someone else that had scuba dived the sink hole. People said there were old cars at the bottom, and catfish the size of Volkswagens. There was even a rumour that an old steamboat sank down there. There were supposedly slot machines full of coins and tables with poker chips still piled high waiting to be claimed.

They would send the ROV all the way to the bottom and attempt to hold position while they drove the boat in a circle. This would test how well it could stabilize itself in a strong current. They all agreed on the plan except Jose, who only agreed as long as it was okay if he fished.

They pulled away from the dock and headed down the river. When they arrived at the sink hole, Cody shut off the engine. They waited to see how strong the current would be since they planned on not anchoring at first. To their surprise the water was almost dead still. There was a little current but it was very slow. They only moved about a foot or two in a minute.

Cody pulled the arm for the hoist and lifted the ROV over the edge. Brian put a hand on it to keep it from spinning.

"So, how's this shit work? You just drop it in the water and drive it around like a drone?" Mark asked as he flicked his cigarette into the water.

"Pretty much. Hey, don't put that shit in the water. Use a soda can or something," Cody stated as his friend flicked cigarette ash into the water. "Anyway, once it's in the water, we can control it from the helm and monitor the cameras."

"Yo, can I drive this thing?" Mark followed up.

"Yeah, I don't see why not. As soon as the gyro is calibrated, and I get it free from anything it could potentially get snagged on. And assuming you don't throw more trash in the water," Cody explained in a jovial jest.

The ROV splashed down and they started calibrating the gyroscope. They drove it in a couple small circles, and did a few rolls to make sure the controls functioned properly. The ROV dove toward the sinkhole and cable spun violently from the reel. Then, the entire world seemed to drop away.

The water in the river was much darker than the water in the sinkhole. It was stained a dark brown by the tannins of the forest and tree roots from the surrounding swamp.

Inside of Buffalo Breakdown, the water was a clear blue. This was because the water in the sinkhole came from an underground spring, visibility changing from about five to ten feet to an impressive hundred feet or so. It wasn't perfect. The dark blanket of the coffee colored water above blocked most of the sunlight from reaching the bottom. They could see a long way down the wall of the breakdown. Then Cody turned on the lights. Now they could see a hundred feet ahead.

The impressive size of the sink hole came into view. Even with the impressive visibility and the bright lights they couldn't see the bottom or the far side. Cody stepped away from the helm and gestured to the controls for his friends to try. Mark shook his head.

"Nah, Brian should go next. He was the one who designed and printed most of it. He should go," Mark explained.

Brian took a long drag from his vape, and with a beaming smile, placed his hands on the controls. They had mapped the ROV controls to be the same as one of the flying games they all played together. He tilted the ROV toward the bottom and looked toward Cody for approval. Cody nodded and he sent the ROV into the depths. Now they were going to find out the truth about those rumors.

Chapter Two

Wendy

Further up the river a group of college students were celebrating the conclusion of the semester. The smell of beer wafted through the air, as laughter echoed across the water and back from the steeply sloped bank.

One of the guys floating in an inner tube tossed a football toward the bow of their boat. Another one jumped into the water, catching the ball midair. Everyone cheered. Drinks, jokes, and gossip flowed like a torrent in the wake of their fun and games. A bag of chimps crinkled and crunched as one of them reached into it.

"What are your plans for next semester?" Sarah asked.

"I'm not sure. I think I might change my major to focus on Biology. I heard about a study abroad program that I could qualify for. I need to up my GPA though. I'm like, right on the cusp. I want to make sure I can get in," Wendy replied.

"That sounds really fun. Where would you go?"

"Peru. We would get to study the jungle and visit one of the archeology sites there. It will be for six weeks though."

"Damn! I won't be able to see you for six weeks? That's going to suck. You better have a lot of fun for me while you're over there."

"I will. You keep an eye on Luke for me. It's not that I don't trust him. He just has a way of getting himself in trouble you know?"

"Yeah, I get it. That boy is a hazard. How long have you two been together now?"

"Ten years in May."

"Wow. I'm surprised he hasn't gotten himself killed or arrested in that time."

"Sarah!"

"Sorry, it's true, honey. I'm glad you two are happy and all, but why him?"

"He's the one that I love. We were meant for each other. That's all there is to it. You remember last year when my uncle passed away and we had to board his expensive ass horse until we could sell him?" Sarah replied.

"Yeah."

"Well...it was Luke that took care of him, cleaned his stall, fed him, rode him, and groomed him. He had no obligation whatsoever. He knew I was overworked as it was. He did all of that while working doubles and saving up money for us to have our own place."

"Yeah, a place in the worst part of town where he never stays. Speaking of which, why couldn't he make it today?"

"He's working, busting his ass so we can afford a house."

"Wendy, you could do so much better. Teddy is crazy about you. C'mon, the Mayor's son...he's in law school, and already has a job lined up at his father's firm. Why don't you at least talk to him? You and Luke were cute in high school. But it's time to grow up now."

"If Teddy is so great, why don't you date him?"

"That's not what I meant. Please don't take it that way. I'm just saying keep your options open. I'm just trying to look out for you. Luke is a trouble maker. Who knows how long until he gets himself into something he can't handle."

"Well, maybe you should look out for yourself. I think you're right though, I do need to grow up. I need to stop hanging out with immature people who think they know everything."

"Damn it, Wendy. You just don't have a clue do you?"

"I'd rather be clueless than stuck up."

Wendy stormed off and didn't give Sarah a chance to say much of anything else back. She was pissed. She knew Sarah didn't like Luke, but this was too much. She looked down the river and thought about swimming back to her car. That's when she saw something moving under the water's surface. It was far away. It didn't look like an alligator. It was definitely big though.

Teddy stumbled into Wendy and spilled his beer all over her.

"Oh shit! Sorry...I didn't mean to."

"It's fine."

"Let me get a towel. I'll help you clean up."

"No, seriously it's fine. I was about to jump in the water anyway."

Wendy pushed past Teddy and walked to the ladder on the side of the pontoon boat. She climbed down and settled into the water. Her mind went back to the large shape she saw in the earlier. She wondered if it was a manatee. She loved manatees. They were one of the reasons she wanted to be a biologist.

She swam over to the large tree hanging over the water. She wanted to climb up to the rope swing and jump off from the top.

Wendy climbed the tree and by the time she reached the top she had forgotten all about her argument with Sarah. She looked out over the river and scanned the surface for any sign of manatees, but she didn't see anything. She looked down at the boat, smiling,wondering if she could splash and soak Teddy as pay back for the beer. One good well-timed cannon ball should do it.

She watched patiently waiting for the perfect moment to strike. The branch she was on was about twenty feet up and hung a good forty feet toward the middle of the river. She saw Teddy start walking toward the cooler.

This was perfect.

She would wait until he opened his new beer.

Just as she was about to jump. Someone screamed from behind her. She couldn't see what had happened, but the water had turned red. A group of people were frantically swimming away from the blood clouded water. Then in front of her she heard a banging and yelling.

Some of the people in tubes around the pontoon were trying to climb up onto the boat. Some of the guys on the smaller john boat were slapping the water and pounding their fists on the side of the boat to try and distract the large animal so the swimmers could get out of the water. In their panicked rush, the swimmers ended up pulling more people into the water. Everyone was panicking in the pandemonium. A group of jet skiers took off up the river.

"Jesus, I hope they're going for help."

"Wendy! Wendy! WEEENDY!!!" Sarah called out.

"I'm up here! I got in the tree before the attack started! What happened? What is it?"

"I don't know it's big though! It got Derek!"

"Stay there. I'm calling for help."

Sarah had her phone in her hand when one of the younger boys that looked about thirteen started screaming for help. He was trying to climb up the back of the boat. Sarah leaned over while she tried to help the boy on board. The back of the boat was hard to get a grip on.

Sarah climbed over the rail and stood next to the motor. She crouched down and started to pull the boy up. Then Wendy saw the large wake of the creature turn towards them.

"Sarah! It's coming! Hurry!" Wendy cried to her friend.

Sarah looked up and her eyes doubled in size when she saw it heading for her. As the boy climbed aboard, Sarah lost her balance. She fell halfway in and hit her side on the edge of the transom. It looked really painful.

Wendy watched in terror as the giant beast raced toward Sarah. Sarah got her wits about her. She wanted to look behind her to see how far away the creature was, but she knew she didn't have time to look. She grabbed and clawed at the boat but her hands didn't grab anything solid.

The boy leaned over and tried to pull Sarah up. He wasn't strong enough on his own. Sarah slipped right through his fingers and splashed back into the water. The boy turned around and grabbed a net. He placed it over the first thing he saw and handed the other end to Sarah.

Sarah grabbed the handle and pulled. She got her feet on top of the transom. Wendy watched as the enormous wake grew closer, and the water splashed and broke into frothy waves behind it.

"Sarah! Hurry! it's almost there!"

Sarah pulled as hard as she could. She lifted herself up out of the water and the younger boy helped her into the boat.

Then the creature slammed into the side of the boat. The platform of the pontoon cracked and splinters flew through the air. The pontoon boat started to sag in the middle but it stayed a float.

Wendy breathed a sigh of relief. At the front of the pontoon boat there was a group of swimmers fighting over each other to get into the relative safety of the crumpled up boat. Teddy leaned over the front of the boat and tried to help one of his friends get out of the water. There was another scream from behind Wendy. The scream was cut off with a gurgling and a splash. Everyone was screaming and splashing around. There was even more blood filling the water now. It was chaos.

Wendy looked back at the boat. A giant pair of long, toothy jaws sprang from the water and snatched Teddy from the front of the boat. When the monster came down on the boat it ripped the pontoon in two pieces. People frantically clung to what bits of debris and flotsam they could find. Then Wendy started to feel the tree shaking. People were trying to climb out of the water and into the tree.

A large, spiny dorsal fin cut through the water and aimed straight for the people trying to get on the tree. The creature sped up, dragging a massive wake behind it.

Then its head broke the surface and its large, long, snaggle-toothed jaws snapped down on two of the swimmers.

The tree shook violently. It grabbed the tire swing that hung just above the water during its ravenous frenzy. Wendy started to hear the tree creaking and cracking. Then there was a loud snap, and the branch she was sitting on collapsed into the water. She felt like she had fallen a hundred feet.

When she hit the water, she was in a wash of bubbles and agitated water. She kicked violently for the surface as she struggled to hold onto the half breath she was able to grab before she was completely submerged.

Finally, her head broke the surface, and she whipped up in a full panic. Her eyes darted around for anything that could save her. She saw Sarrah clinging to a large board still partially floating. Wendy paddled over as fast as she could and tried to climb on. As she did the board flipped over and now both of them were in the water and in severe danger. Alice clambered on top of the board and felt something grab her.

"Wait! Help me up!"

It was Sarah. Her hand was on Wendy's shoulder. Wendy needed to get to safety. She would help Sarah once she was safe herself.

"Let me get on! I'll help you up once I'm on."

Sarah didn't like that answer. She dug her nails into Wendy's back. Wendy kicked Sarah off of her and finished climbing onto the debris. She turned to offer Sarah a hand but it was too late. She watched helplessly as Sarah was exenterated.

Chapter Three

Cody

Cody was chewing a mouthful of PB&J as he watched Mark pilot the ROV toward the opening of a large underwater cave.

"Is it cool if I go inside?" Mark asked.

"I'd be more upset if you didn't. It's what it was made for. Send it!" Cody explained.

"Full steam ahead, Captain," Brian said.

After exploring the bottom of the sink hole, they found almost none of the fabled goodies. What they had found was an old pick-up truck, no cat fish, and the very rotted remains of what might have been a steamboat a hundred years ago. They began to look for something else more interesting.

The ROV entered the cave and hovered slowly inside the cavern area of it. From there, the back of the cave opened up into a giant chamber. It was big enough to fit a tractor trailer inside. You could probably even turn the truck around in there. The room ended in a fisher that slowly got narrower as it went.

Mark pushed further into the cave. As he passed through the fisher, it started to close in from the ceiling and floor, then started to widen slightly. The ROV continued deeper into the cave. The cave continued until it split into a fork. There was one opening to the bottom right that looked too small for the ROV to fit through. Then there was an over under opening to the left. The one on the bottom was wider than it was tall. The one on the upper left was just as wide as the one below it but the top continued up as it got more and more narrow.

"Go through the top one and it looks really cool!" Cody said excitedly.

"What if the bottom one keeps going deeper though?" Brian questioned aloud.

"Yeah it looks like it points down. We should do that one," said Jose as he looked over his shoulder while reeling in his lure.

"I didn't think about that. That does sound cooler. You should go up though. There might be cool shit in there," Cody explained.

"Down it is! Hahaha."

Mark steered the ROV down and through the passage. It started to spiral down as it went, making it more and more difficult for Mark to maneuver.

"You know...I gotta say, I thought this thing would be way harder to drive. It's really fuck'n easy actually."

"That was the idea. We wanted to make sure it not only felt like it could pilot itself, but it actually could as a fail safe."

"That's fucking cool as shit."

Mark gently eased the ROV deeper until it stopped and started to turn and spin. The cable had gotten stuck. A giant cloud of silt billowed up from the bottom and wrecked the visibility.

"Shit! I can't see a fucking thing! What do we do now?"

"Oh shit! Are we fucked?" Jose asked worriedly.

Everyone seemed on edge. They were all worried that Cody's money and hard work was now stuck in an underwater cave permanently.

"Nothing to worry about guys. I built a feature just for this potential issue."

Cody hopped up, leaned over the key board and held control-alt-D. Then the Spool and ROV started to move in unison.

"I programmed a revert dive function. It makes a sonar map of its surroundings while it's operating. Now it can back itself out slowly in the event of an emergency. As long as the cable isn't physically stuck we should be good to go. If it is. We will just wait for the visibility to clear up, but it should be able to back itself out on its own."

"So, if it's making a sonar map the whole time it's underwater, can we see the map?" Mark asked.

"Well, I can show you the map. I'm afraid it wouldn't make much sense though. I can enter the coordinates into Google Earth and show you a map that way. That is easy enough to automate. I haven't done it yet though. But the sonar map is just a bunch of data points. Like I said, I could show it to you, but it would just look like a bunch of numbers and symbols.

I'm working on a program that can make a visual map with that data. There are programs available that will do it for you but they are expensive. They don't integrate with the transducer I have either. I don't want to buy a ten thousand dollar transducer just so I can use someone else's software more easily. I can figure it out, so that I can use a cheaper program to generate the sonar visualization. It's going to take time though. The cool thing is that once I can figure it out, I should be able to use all of the data I already have recorded."

"That's really cool," Jose exclaimed

"How the fuck did you figure all this shit out?" Mark asked.

"Lot's of research," Cody answered.

The ROV backed out of the cave and everyone was able to see again. The swirling mass of dark silt writhed inside of the cave opening. Cody leaned over the keyboard again, hit control-alt-C, and the ROV stopped. Everyone looked around and eyes focused on Jose.

"It's your turn if you want to try it out."

"How can I say no?" Jose answered as he moved behind the keyboard.

As Jose started to play with the ROV, another boat pulled up not far from them. It was a dive boat. They were really common in Buffalo Breakdown. Divers loved exploring the giant sinkhole. Cody watched the divers longingly as they put on their gear. He could tell they were likely cave divers because they were using sidemount tan ks.Cody wished he had binoculars. He wondered if they were diving with Trimix to reach some of the deeper caves.

"Look at that!" Cody exclaimed.

Everyone stared at the monitor with their eyes darting back and forth. Then they realized he was talking about the dive boat.

"That guy has a rebreather!"

One of the divers looked over at Cody and his group and chuckled as he said something to the diver with the rebreather. The diver with the rebreather looked up and waved to Cody.

Cody gave an over exaggerated and pretty embarrassing wave. Everyone else on the boat rolled their eyes in embarrassment for Cody. He wasn't embarrassed at all though. He would have loved to have talked that divers ear off about their rebreather. What they did for diluent, what scrubber media they used, and how the work of breathing was on their particular set up. The rebreather looked like it was homemade. There were very few sidemount rebreathers around.

Cody watched with bated-breath as each diver got into the water. He wondered if they were going into the cave the ROV was just in. He hoped not. The visibility was still trashed in that section.

"Hey, Jose, see if you can get a look at those divers and where they are heading. They might show us a new cave we can check out next time we're here."

"You sure you don't want me to follow them into the cave too?" Jose joked.

"Obviously not. I'm just curious."

"Alright, Captain. It's your boat and your toy. Who am I to judge? If I see some really cool fish I'm chasing after that instead though."

"Deal."

The ROV turned and started off in the direction of the divers. Jose got close enough to see the finer details of their equipment, but it still was hard to see due to the effect of the water.

The divers seemed to notice their pursuer. They each waved and held up the OKAY symbol before continuing their dive. Cody watched with anticipation as he watched the divers make it to their cave and swim inside. Cody didn't want to bother them, so he told Jose he was off the hook. Mark had lit up a fresh cigarette as he turned to look off in the distance.

"Yo! Holy shit! Hey guys, give me a hand here."

The group heard something thud into the boat. They all struggled to keep their footing as Mark bolted to the opposite side. Everyone rushed over as the boat rocked in the water to see what Mark was talking about.

That's when they saw it.

Or more accurately *her.*

She was floating on a piece of plywood, shivering and despondent. The girl had a large gash on her back that curved around to her hip.

Mark and Jose ran over and tried to help the girl up. She jumped and started screaming, flailing around and clawing Mark's face.

Cody ran over and checked on Mark. His face was cut pretty badly. Jose and Brian tried to calm her down but she kept screaming. She fell back into the water and scrambled to get out. Then she begged for help.

Jose and Brian offered their hands wearily, in fear of sharing Mark's fate. The girl ended up climbing aboard. Cody wrapped her in a towel and a blanket. She was shivering even more than she was before.

"You have a really bad cut on your back. I'd like to help you. I need to know you aren't going to hurt me or my friends. My name is Cody. What's your name?"

"Wendy. I won't hurt you if you don't hurt me."

"Deal."

Cody and Mark had first aid training and experience, so they had Wendy lay down so they could clean and bandage the wound on her back.

"How old are you Wendy?"

"I'm twenty years old."

"When is your birthday?"

"Ten sixteen two thousand and six"

"A libra huh?"

"Yep, what's with all the questions?" she asked.

"Just trying to make sure you know who and where you are. I want to make sure you don't have any injuries we can't see. Do you remember what happened before we found you?"

Wendy explained in excruciating detail everything she saw. The guys stared vacantly with their jaws on the floor. They had no idea if she was telling the truth or not. But her story was too intense to ignore. The implication was clear. Something was in the water.

Chapter Four

Alice

As the boat throttled down, the wake pushed up the stern and the boat briefly surfed up the river. Everyone shifted around the boat. The radio was cut off and Danny jumped up to set the anchor line on the bow. He held the anchor and looked back toward Alice waiting for her prompt to drop the anchor.

"Here looks good. Drop it Danny."

Danny threw down the anchor and Alice put the boat in neutral. The boat drifted back downstream and set the anchor. Danny looped the rope on the cleat and cinched it in place.

Satisfied the boat was anchored Alice cut the engine and hopped over the back seat to turn off the battery.

"Alright! Let's do it!" Alice exclaimed.

The sound of clanking tanks, squeaking plastic and neoprene filled the air.

"Looks like we're the only ones here diving. Should be good viz' in the cave for once," Marco stated.

"Yeah as long as Danny the silt monster doesn't attack," Pat said mockingly.

Danny groaned and Marco chuckled.

"Hey at least I didn't spend half my dive surveying a *'new passage'* that already had line in it," Danny fired back.

"I might have seen it if *you* didn't cause a typhoon level silt storm. Seriously, we probably should have reported it to NOAA as a meteorological event."

"Ha, ha-ha ha. Very funny." Danny fake laughed.

"Alright ladies, one more time. Danny is the biggest and has the worst breath rate. Sorry but you are leading. I've got the rebreather, so when we get to Monarch's Meadow we will split up. I'll lead with Pat behind me. We are penetrating deeper, but we will be doing a faster paced dive. Our turn pressure should be about the same as yours. No matter what, we are back on the boat in two hours. No exceptions. Is that clear?"

"It's not fair you and your girly lungs get to go deeper," Marco protested

"Sorry, I didn't mean to rub salt in the wound. I know you have a hard time penetrating very deep," Alice fired back, not taking any prisoners.

The entire ship, except for Marco, laughed at that one.

"Okay everyone, do we all understand and agree with the plan?" Alice asked one more time.

"Aye aye, Capt'n," Pat agreed

"Yep," Marco answered.

Danny grunted and nodded as he clipped his harness. Pat tapped Alice on the shoulder and pointed behind her.

"Look's like you got an admirer. I think he's looking at your rebreather set up."

Alice waved and the guy on the other boat did his best Forest Gump impression. Alice chuckled and recognized the over dramatic wave. She thought it was a little cute.

"What do you think they're up to? Fishing?" Alice asked.

"Probaby. Oh, yeah I just saw one of them casting. You want to fuck with them and put something on one of their hooks?" Pat suggested only half joking.

"Stooop, you play too much."

"Hey, you guys don't think there will be another earthquake do you?" Marco asked.

"Not likely. Nothing's impossible, but it's more likely this is the safest time. The earthquake that happened was so small it was imperceptible," Alice answered.

After everyone was in the water, they all swam down to the opening of the cave. On their way down they heard a strange whirring sound.

Alice looked over when she thought she saw another dive light. She was expecting to see another diver. She was not expecting an entire submarine.

Or was it?

It was an ROV!

That must have been what the other boat was doing. She smiled and turned to wave at it. The rest of the group noticed and waved as well. Seeing a group of side mount divers, especially one with a rebreather, was rare enough. Seeing an ROV was crazy. Alice had to know more about it. She hoped they would still be around when they surfaced.

Danny reached down and tied his spool to a protrusion at the entrance for the cave. The gold colored main line was still about a hundred feet deeper into the cave. Their group always made sure to tie off just in case something went wrong and they needed to feel their way out. Silt outs in the cavern zone of the cave were not uncommon.

In the event of an emergency the last thing you would want is to get lost less than two hundred feet from the surface. Once they were all inside they clipped their pure oxygen decompression tanks to the gold colored main line and placed one non-directional marker, or *cookie,* on the line. Everyone places their own unique marker. This serves two purposes. It lets everyone know who was in the cave, but also if they are still inside the cave.

The cave on this side of Buffalo Breakdown was named Goblins Gullet. The cave was named for the large jagged protrusions that lined the cavern entrance, giving it a fang toothed appearance. The large cavern entrance that reduced down to a narrow restriction gave it an even closer resemblance to a mouth and throat.

Goblins Gullet or GG as most called it was a vast cave system with about four thousand feet of surveyed cave passage. The goal of getting to Monarchs Meadow meant they would have to swim eight hundred feet into the cave. There, the gold line split into two directions. To the left where the boys would be going, was an area called The Throne Room. It was a very large chamber with a large rock formation that resembled a giant king's throne. The room itself was about sixty feet tall and around ninety feet wide. This section of the cave dead ends there. However, there were multiple offshoots on the way there. Those would be off limits for this dive.

The girls would be going to the right. They had a more labor-intensive dive. Pat was the smallest of the group and her breathing rate was low...very low. In diving, it is referred to as having girly lungs. Which is considered a huge compliment. Every diver wishes they could stay down longer. The girls would head down through a corkscrew formation nicknamed The Gauntlet. So named for its aggressive and numerous restrictions, tight corners, and the sheer amount of rubble you had to navigate. It was exhausting and very time consuming. The reward was breathtaking though.

When the sinkhole collapsed and created Buffalo Breakdown, a large void was created beneath. When the earth filled that void, it left a fisher that was about seventy feet wide and stretched down to a jaw dropping five hundred and fifty feet. This section was approximately two hundred feet in length. Many expeditions have attempted to find other ways into the passage. None have been successful. This passage was fittingly named Infinity Deep.

Danny led the group. It was best practice, when cave diving in a group, to have the largest person lead on the way in and be in the back on the way out. that way, if they ended up getting stuck, no one would be trapped behind them.

As they approached the throat of the Goblins Mouth, the current pushed back against them. It wasn't too strong to keep them from entering, but they did have to grab onto the cave to pull themselves in. After they squeezed through, they hovered low and close to the floor of the cave. Once out of the current, they swam through the cave passage just above the guide line.

After about fifteen minutes they came to the first intersection on the guideline. Now they would place a directional marker, followed by a series of cookies on the side of the intersection that they had traveled into. The intersection had a permanent directional marker pointing to the exit.

Everyone took their time.

They enjoyed the scenery but they were all excited to get to their respective destinations. They all knew very well that if they rushed off in a hurry, they would have less air to breathe in the passages they wanted to get to. It was a long and arduous journey to Monarchs Meadow.

When they approached the entrance, the reason for its name was immediately apparent. The restriction to the passage was shaped like a giant butterfly. The room on the other side had a very unique floor. The entire floor was coated in patches of mesolite. Mesolite is a sparkling white and fuzzy mineral often deposited from volcanic flows or hydrothermal vents. It gave the cave the appearance of a frost covered meadow. It was one of the best kept secrets in all of cave diving. Few people knew of its existence and it was a close guarded secret. Everyone slowed down and shone their lights around to admire the spectacle that was Monarchs Meadow.

Then Alice covered and uncovered her dive light to get everyone's attention. They shielded their dive lights and focused on Alice. She held up the okay sign to make sure everyone was ready to split up. Marco and Danny agreed, then Pat did the same. Marco and Danny didn't have far to go. They placed their markers on their side of the T intersection and swam down the passage. Alice and Pat did the same on their side. They made it to The Gauntlet and began the challenging descent. Alice led the way. Her rebreather was larger than Pat's side mount even with her extra stage tank.

Alice was a little nervous. She slowed her breathing and focused on the task at hand. She had navigated this section multiple times before. This was her first time doing it with her rebreather though. She had to be careful to keep her breathing rate steady. If you breathe too quickly with a rebreather, you can create more carbon-dioxide than the system can handle. That would cause her to take a carbon-dioxide hit which would be fatal in this environment. The air we breathe above the water contains approximately twenty one percent oxygen. And point ninety three percent carbon dioxide.

In a rebreather, the oxygen is closer to sixteen percent. Carbon-dioxide should stay below two percent for safety. This is considered the maximum threshold for safety, but it is desired to be as close to zero as possible. At five to seven percent carbon-dioxide the feeling can be equated to having too many beers. Prolonged exposure at these levels can lead to headaches, disorientation, and eventually a loss of consciousness. A carbon dioxide hit of thirty percent will cause a diver to pass out within one to two breaths. Passing out underwater equals death.

As Alice carefully negotiated the corkscrew passage of The Gauntlet, she made sure to avoid touching the floor to preserve the visibility for Pat. Pat was behind Alice. She was keeping up a good pace. Even better than that, Pat wasn't disturbing the silt at all. Alice made it to the smallest restriction between her and Infinity Deep. She swam into the restriction slowly and tried to turn slightly.

She felt her diluent tank scrape and she stopped in place. She exhaled and sucked in her tummy and wiggled. She slid forward slightly, then she stopped. She wiggled her hips and gained only about an inch this time. Alice was calm, she still wasn't stuck. She was making progress. Slow progress, but progress.

She shifted her shoulders and tried to shimmy.

Nothing.

She took a few breaths and tried to stay cool and collected. She shook her hips and tried to rotate her body.

Nothing.

She tried to back up and reposition.

She didn't budge.

Now she was officially stuck. She reached down between her and the cave, then ran her fingers along her equipment trying to find where she might be stuck. She pulled her hands back out and wiggled again. It felt like she was getting caught on her buttplate.

She reached back behind her buoyancy control device and felt around. The canister for her divelight had become wedged in a depression in the rock. She felt around for the velcro strap that held the canister in place. She found it and pulled it apart. The canister shifted slightly and she was able to push forward. She scraped and got caught up slightly once more on the way through, but she made it.

Once on the other side she re-affixed her divelight canister and waited for Pat to make sure she made it through as well. Pat was diving asidemount configuration, and her smaller profile made it through the restriction with much less difficulty.

Most divelights these days no longer require a separate canister for the batteries. Canister lights are more popular with older divers. New divers tend to prefer the simplicity of having the battery and buttons near the light itself. Alice preferred her old canister light because of how long she had been using it, how familiar she was with it, and the added weight to her butt plate helped her achieve perfect trim. It was just something she had grown to prefer.

The rest of The Gauntlet put up little fight compared to the restriction earlier. Once inside Infinity Deep, Alice checked her dive computer. It had been forty five minutes since they started their dive. They would have about twenty minutes to explore before turning around. They were one hundred and eighty feet deep and Pat wouldn't be able to stay for long.

Alice scanned the area ahead with her dive light. The bottom was a black abyss that continued on for what seemed like eternity. The wall to the left went as far as she could see. The wall to her right was almost out of sight. It was just shy of being past how far her light could illuminate.

Pat made her way out of the restriction and they began their exploration. Now Alice would lead the way. The guideline in this section of the cave stayed at one hundred and eighty feet of depth. It hugged the left wall and as they continued, it got further and further from the ceiling.

Alice looked down and noticed the opening to a cave passage. She clipped her explorer reel to the line. Eager for the opportunity to lay a line in a virgin cave passage, she descended down. Pat stayed close behind but did not enter the passage. The opening was about eight feet wide and resembled the shape of an avocado.

Alice shined her light inside and saw the passage had no line. Her heart started to thump excitedly. She tied off to a protrusion at the entrance and let out line from her dive reel as she made her way in deeper. She saw something drooping down from the ceiling. She felt the blood in her veins run cold.

At first when she saw one of the flippers, she thought it might be a diver. She relaxed a little when she realized it wasn't a diver. As she traced her light over the object, it became obvious it was a manatee. Her heart sank.

The poor thing must have wandered into the cave and got lost, she thought to herself.

Then her light stopped on a portion of the manatee that was wrong. Her heart began to race. The manatee had a large bite in its mid section. All of the organs seemed to be missing. There were scrape marks on some of the bones. Something big was eating this manatee. It made no sense. Her mind rushed with possible answers. None of them made sense. It couldn't be a reptile. It was way too cold. A shark made the most sense but no shark big enough to eat a manatee would be in this cave. The body seemed to be deliberately placed here—saved for later.

A chill ran down her spine. It was time to go.

As Alice turned, she heard a loud thud and the sound of twigs snapping. She knew something bad had just happened. She shined her divelight around frantically but couldn't see anything.

Something was off.

She couldn't hear Pat's regulator anymore. Underwater sound travels farther and faster. Unfortunately, sound is not directional underwater. She knew something had happened. She had no way of knowing which direction though. Slowly she exited the cave passage. It was time to end the dive and head back. She looked around for Pat and didn't see her anywhere.

She stopped, slowed her breathing and listened for her regulator. Nothing, no sound, no bubbles, no dive light. She shielded her dive light and waited a moment for her eyes to adjust. She looked around again. Straight down she saw a faint flickering glow.

Alice freed her dive line from the cave passage and swam straight down. She checked her dive computer. Two hundred and twenty feet. She was reaching the limit of how far Pat could dive. The glow was getting closer. It flickered and strobed creating a shudder affect before her eyes. She swam down. The light flickered, she saw the rocks on the bottom and something strewn amongst them. Then darkness. It flashed again. She saw one of Pat's tanks. Then darkness. Then it flashed again. One of Pat's flippers was floating up still attached to whatever was still attached to the tank. Then darkness.

Alice was finning as fast as she could. The light flashed again and Alice could briefly understand what she was looking at. Pat's leg was partially attached to the tank by a piece of her wetsuit snagged on the hose clamp attached to the tank. A few pieces of other gear had sunk and fallen amongst the rocks. It was clear that Pat was no longer alive.

As the darkness closed in again, something rushed past Alice. The light flashed again. Something massive was between her and the light now. Alice stopped. Then it was dark again. Alice turned—she had to escape.

She unclipped and tossed her explorer reel. She tugged at the line as she swam up in a mad dash for the cave opening. Alice could hear her dive computer start to beep.

She didn't need to look—she knew she was overexerting herself. She spit out the mouthpiece of the rebreather and bit down on the regulator for her bailout tank. She kicked her legs with everything she had.

Yanking and tugging herself up the line until she got back to the guideline, Alice swam hard for the narrow restriction leading into The Gauntlet. She crashed into the opening trying to get in. She pulled herself down onto the guideline and tried to pull herself in again. This time she was successful. She made it in and turned to look if she was being pursued by a giant predator.

There was nothing there.

Alice's vision began to fade. That's when she realized she had been crying. She cleared her mask and checked her bailout tank's pressure gauge. Twenty seven hundred PSI. She had breathed through eight hundred PSI during her mad dash from Infinity Deep. She should still have enough to get back to her decompression tank. She still had her rebreather but the risk of getting a carbon-dioxide hit was too high to try and breathe from it.

Alice flushed the rebreather with diluent and started swimming back to Monarch's Meadow. When she made it back she would double check the level of carbon-dioxide in the rebreather on her divecomputer. If everything looked okay she could switch back to the rebreather. She had to focus on getting back to the meadow. With any luck, Marco and Danny hadn't started their exit yet.

Alice squeezed back through The Gauntlet. She got hung up on her rebreather hose going through one of the narrow passages. It did little to slow her down though. She made it back to The Meadow and raced toward the line markers. Her hand went out as she went to grab Pat's. She stopped and brushed her thumb against the initials P.F. and left the marker in place.

She was happy to see Marco and Danny hadn't left yet. She looked at her dive computer. The oxygen meter in her rebreather was reading safe. She purged the regulator and took a breath from her rebreather. The air felt good. She would be vigilant for a headache, any dizziness, or disorientation. She checked the regulator on her bailout tank—nineteen hundred PSI, which was plenty for now.

After assessing all of her gear Alice pulled out her wet notes. She would need to explain what had happened to Pat. She thought for a moment. Then she scribbled on the page. As she was writing, she saw the dive lights of Marco and Danny emerge from the passage. They arrived just as she had finished. They were clearly confused about the absence of Pat. Alice held out her wet notes.

"*PATS DEAD, ANIMAL ATTACK. SURFACE NOW!!!*"

Danny's eyes almost exploded out of his mask as he looked toward the passage leading to The Gauntlet. Marco snatched the notes from Danny and read the message.

Alice saw his face turn red. She wasn't sure if it was sadness or anger, but there was a lot of whichever emotion it was.

Marco and Pat weren't dating but they had hooked up more than once. They were more than just friends, and it was clear that it hurt him deeply. They collected their line markers. Marco didn't hesitate; he took Pat's line marker and tucked it into his wet suit. They continued on their way out of the cave.

Chapter Five

Cody

Everyone was shocked by Wendy's story. Mark pulled Cody to the side.

"Hey, we have to get this chick to the hospital. It doesn't matter if her story is for real or not. We don't want to get mixed up in whatever the fuck happened upriver."

"I don't disagree, but we need to call nine-one-one and report this to the cops or the Coast Guard. I don't really know. We can't afford to do things the wrong way. More people might need help."

"It's your boat, dude. But I think we should get to shore as soon as possible. This chick is going to be nothing but trouble for us," Mark suggested.

"We'll pull up the ROV and head for the dock while we call the cops," Cody stated.

While they were talking, Brian had already called nine-one-one and was talking with the dispatcher. Cody started pulling up the ROV when he noticed the dive boat. They were still down there. Cody didn't know what to do. He felt like he had to do something to warn the divers.

"Hey! Hold on. What about the divers? If they're still down there, they'll be sitting ducks. We can't just leave them here without at least warning them."

"What do you want to do?" Brian asked.

"I don't know. Tell the cops what's happening and ask them what we should do. Tell them we have an extremely sophisticated submarine. Emphasize that it is not a toy."

Brian relayed the information. Then there was a lot of, "Yep, no, u-huh, yes, and no." He looked at Wendy.

"How do you feel? Do you want immediate medical attention?"

"I want to know my friends are safe. If there are more people that need our help, we should help them."

Brian explained more of the situation to the dispatcher. Everyone waited with bated-breath, then he hung up the phone.

"Okay, they said Marine Patrol is on the way. They want us to stay put. They want to do an investigation. They said for everyone to stay out of the water. If it is a dangerous animal, they said for us to keep our distance and try to scare it away if it starts to get too close. They said Marine Patrol Eighteen is twenty minutes out. They want us to tune to channel sixty eight on our radio."

"Okay, hang on," Mark spoke up. "They want us to stay put? Wendy said that thing turned a pontoon boat into a pile of fucking mulch. I think we should get the fuck out of here."

"We need to do this by the book. I've gone my entire life without any trouble with the law. I'm not going to start now. Not to mention there are people that need our help," Cody said with a tone of finality.

"This is fucking stupid. I'm telling you this is bad news. Do whatever you want, it's your boat," Mark said in return.

Cody grabbed the radio and tuned it to channel sixty eight.

"Marine Patrol Eighteen, this is the Diligaf, do you copy? Over."

"This is Marine Patrol Eighteen. We copy. Can you tell us a little of what's going on? Over."

Cody brought Marine Patrol up to speed and said he would update them if anything changed. He set down the radio and went back to the ROV controls.

"I'm sending the ROV down to warn the divers. We need some way to tell them what's going on. Any ideas?" Cody asked.

"We need something to write on and with," Brian stated.

"I've got pen and paper, but it's not going to work underwater," Cody explained.

"I know, just give me something to write with."

Cody handed him the pen and paper. Then he started writing the message. The message was short and to the point.

Dangerous animal. Use extreme caution. Follow sub.

"What do you think?" Brian asked.

"It makes sense, we can lead the way or get in between the thing and them if need be. How are we going to make sure they can see it though?"

Brian reached into the trash and pulled out the resealable bag that once held the PB&J Cody ate earlier. He stuffed the note inside and squeezed out the air as much as possible.

"There is no guarantee it will work, but it's the best we've got I think," Brian explained.

"Let's send it down."

Brian leaned over the edge of the boat and held out the note for the ROV to grab in its manipulator arm. The manipulator closed on the note and Cody sent it into the water to where they last saw the divers. The ROV descended toward the cave opening. There was no sign of the divers. They decided to wait. Cody used the ROV's other manipulator to grab onto a protrusion outside of the cave. Once the ROV had a firm grip he turned off the motors to conserve energy. Then they waited.

"What are we going to tell the cops when they get here?" Jose asked.

"How about the truth?" Wendy answered.

"You want to go to the mental hospital? I hope you're ready to take a sobriety test after you share your little story," Mark explained.

"Okay, then what do you suggest?" Wendy asked indignantly.

"We tell them there was an animal attack. You couldn't tell what it was. It was big, and very aggressive. Maybe like a hippo or something? I don't know just don't say *giant fucking murder manatee.* I don't think that will go over well for you. You do you though," Mark reasoned.

"Fine, I'll be vague," Wendy answered begrudgingly.

"Where do you think it came from?" Jose asked.

"Who the fuck knows?" Mark answered.

"What if it came from Bridgemont?" Brian suggested.

"Wait, do you think Oscar n' Mandrill have something to do with it?" Mark said with surprise.

"Them or Desanto. It could have mutated from the chemical run off from all the crazy pesticides and God knows what else they've dumped in the water. We've all heard about the cancer clusters. That's just the humans who live near the water. Think about the animals living in the water y'know?" Brian explained further.

"Dude, could you fucking imagine if this thing was the result of some crazy experiment or mutation caused by their hazardous waste shit? Bro, if this gets traced back to them we can kiss our asses goodbye. Have you seen the body counts associated with whistle blowers from those companies? Fuck'n insane you know what I'm sayin?" Mark piled on.

"Okay, can we talk about something else? I just saw people I know get fucking eaten. I'd like to not think about where the monster that did it might have come from...or the impending death from being a witness to something I shouldn't have seen," Wendy said, whispering the last part under her breath.

"Looks like you've got your wish. The divers are exiting the cave!"

Cody watched with bated-breath, hoping the divers would understand the S.O.S. signal from the ROV's lights. At first he thought they were just going to swim right past. The diver with the rebreather seemed very upset at the ROV's presence. Then the diver with the rebreather swam forward. Cody watched as she reached out and grabbed the note. He hoped that it was still legible. The confusion on her face made him think it wasn't. Then he saw her write something down and hold it up to the camera. He couldn't see it very well but he saw 25' and 15'. He assumed those were decompression stops.

Cody decided she must have gotten the gist. He released the wall and nodded the ROV in reply. He slowly led them to their anchor line, watching with the rear facing camera to make sure they didn't get too far away. When he got to the anchor line he ascended and stopped when his depth gauge read twenty-five feet. He supposed they would probably do the decompression stops on the anchor line to maintain depth. He was right in that assumption.

Cody ogled the rebreather in an almost perverse manner. He was a massive nerd for diving. Much to his amazement the rebreather looked like it was homemade. It was impossible to tell other than the fact that it was designed for side mount and didn't resemble any of the models he knew of. Not that there were that many. He marveled at the liberties its creator had taken. Whoever made it knew what they were doing and was very clever. The way the hoses were routed and the type of hoses they had used was genius. They used asymmetrical tubing that contoured with the body as opposed to round hoses. Everything was as streamlined as possible. There was nothing dangling or unsecured. The way everything was routed was a work of art.

Cody noticed at this moment she was eyeing the ROV up and down. Cody felt naked. His ROV was a monument to brute force and function over form. The divers' rebreather looked like the engine compartment of a German sports car. It was dizzying to look at, but it screamed efficiency and deliberate intention. Cody could get lost for hours trying to understand every part of it. He had no such time however.

The marine patrol stole his attention with a loud "*ER-RRT ERRRT*" sounding from its direction. Brian and Mark were waving for the boat's attention. The boat pulled alongside and the officer flipped its bumpers over the gunwale.

"Gentlemen, I'm going to toss you a couple lines. Please tie them off to your vessel."

Cody and Brian caught the ropes and looped them around the cleats of the boat.

"My name is Officer Garcia, and this is Officer Garagan. I'm about to come aboard your vessel. Do you have your registration?"

"Yeah I've got it right here. I have two fire extinguishers. One on the front right, and one near the engine. We've all got PFDs, and I have a throwable next to the front fire extinguisher as you can see. I have a flare gun, and an air horn right here," Cody explained as he handed the registration to the officer.

The other officer climbed aboard and asked to see the recovered castaway. Garcia returned to his patrol boat. Garagan tended to Wendy. Officer Garagan went over the basics of rendering first aid with Wendy. Satisfied with her mental faculties, Garagan pulled out a small note pad and started asking questions.

"Okay, Ms. Valentine, start from the beginning. What happened today?" Garagan asked.

"Me and my friends were having a party upriver. I'm not exactly sure where, I just know it had a rope swing."

"Was anyone drinking?"

"Are you kidding me? Fucking everyone was. There were drugs too. Yes, there was underage drinking as well. I had a seltzer but just one. I didn't take any seasick pills, though I was worried about getting seasick. I'll blow or whatever you need me to do. I just want to make sure people are getting the help they need."

"I'm not worried about testing you. I want to make sure we know as much as possible so we can help your friends. I want to make sure we understand the potential danger."

Wendy looked at Cody then Mark. She looked back at officer Garagan.

"I don't know what it was, but something attacked someone. Everyone started freaking out. Then I turned to look at what was happening..."

Cody was half listening as Wendy recounted her story again. It was only slightly modified. The only thing she really changed was the description of the monster.

Instead, she said things like, "*I didn't get a good look at it.*" or "*It was far away, I couldn't really tell.*"

Cody felt like she was doing a good job. He hoped there was more than one Marine Patrol looking into the matter. The situation didn't sound good.

Cody watched Officer Garcia as he ran his information. Then he remembered the divers. He ran over to the monitor and didn't see the divers anywhere. Cody's heart was racing as he searched with the ROV for any sign of the divers. Where could they have gone? Was Wendy's story true?

Then he looked up and he remembered they had multiple decompression obligations. They were there just as before only slightly higher up the rope. He raised the ROV to where they were. It was so close to the surface he wondered why they stopped at all.

As he got to where they were he focused on the divers. He could see them pretty well but not much else. Then Garcia called for his attention. Cody walked over and answered politely.

"Okay, Mister Reynolds. Everything checks out. Here's your documents back. That's a pretty sophisticated piece of equipment there," Garcia said as he gestured with Cody's documents before handing them back to him.

"Thanks, we made it ourselves."

"Really? Hmm, that's impressive. What are your plans with it? If you don't mind me asking"

Cody smiled.

"I don't mind at all. It's pretty straight forward really. I can't scuba dive due to medical restrictions, so...I made this as sort of the next best thing."

"Scuba diving without getting wet? That's interesting. Do you have a card or contact info? Would you be interested in working with the state from time to time?"

"I would be very interested." Cody handed Garcia one of his business cards.

"That's my day job. Number still works though," Cody explained.

He moved over to the controls of the ROV. The visibility was even worse than before. He lowered the ROV out of the tannin layer. Settled lower he was able to see much further.

"What are you looking at right now?" Garcia asked.

"Well right now we have a group of divers in the water, with a potentially dangerous animal in the water with them. I want to keep an eye out. At least try and put the ROV between it and them if I can. Are you the only one dispatched to this incident?"

"Unfortunately, we are the only one for now. Other boats are on the way but we are the closest. It looks like the girl is refusing medical service. Normally, we would offer her a ride back too, but if she refuses that's her choice, so long as you don't mind. Usually, I would insist but, we have multiple reports of something happening upriver. As soon as we are done here we need to head up there. That's very respectable protecting the divers with your ROV. We could use more people like you on the water."

"I'm here and able to help. They have no way of knowing what's going on. It seemed like the right thing to do. I figured you would be in more of a hurry to get upriver. Wendy made it sound like a lot more people were injured."

"There are, and they have multiple reported dead. Fire Rescue is already on scene though. They have the helicopter, as well as their own boats. We are responding to conduct an investigation. Most likely a crime was committed, either someone molesting an alligator or even a manatee. People don't realize it, but manatees can easily kill you when they are scared. I've seen it before."

"Do you really think it could be a manatee? What about a shark? Do they ever come this far upriver?"

"I'm just guessing based on the little information I've heard. But it is a possibility. As for sharks? Yes, they do wander up here sometimes. It's very rare and usually only nurse sharks. They don't come this far up though. That would probably have to be a bull shark. However, Great Whites have been known to go very far upriver at times. If a Great White was ill or confused and over stimulated, it could be pretty bad in a space as confined as the river."

"That's a scary thought. Do you..." Cody trailed off as he saw a large wake emerge from the opposite side of the sink hole.

Garcia saw Cody's expression change and turned around. His expression said everything. Garcia's face took on a stern and inquisitive quality. He looked at Cody then at the ROV monitor.

"I think it might be time to see what that sub of yours can do my friend. Garagan, It's time to cast off. We need to be ready," Garcia said.

Cody turned his attention back to the controls and thrust the ROV toward the wake. Garargan leapt into action and freed the lines holding the boats together. She held the last line taught as she prepared to board Marine Patrol Vessel Eighteen.

She stepped across the gunwale and settled into MP18. She pulled the bumpers in and took her place behind the helm. The wake was big. Too big and too fast to be a gator. Cody thought Garcia's idea of a lost Great White might not be far from the truth. Then the animal's back broke the water's surface. What appeared to be the dorsal fin was spined and spanned across the most of its back. The spines were connected by a grey membranous skin. It was not a shark of any kind. If it wasn't for the fin and the sheer size of the thing, he would've thought it was a manatee.

He looked back at the ROV monitor and focused on trying to distract the animal. The animal was massive. Cody couldn't see it perfectly in the shallow tannin layer. He could tell it was enormous though. Its tail was shaped more like that of a whale than a manatee. It had much longer flippers that looked more like spined pectoral fins.

Cody got right under the animal and rammed it with the ROV. The response was immediate. Cody hadn't even turned around to lead it away when the thing roared. The water rippled and splashed upward just from the sound alone. The boat rumbled and shook. Cody led the beast away from the divers and hoped he was able to keep it occupied long enough for them to get out of the water.

As he focused on distracting the monster an ear-splitting crack rang through the air. The world seemed to rumble once more from the monster's thunderous roar. Cody looked up and saw Garcia aiming the smoking barrel of a rifle toward the beast. The thing was no longer on the surface. Cody couldn't see it from the ROV either. Cody snapped his vision over to the dive boat. He was relieved to see the divers pulling themselves out of the water. Then he watched as Garcia and Garagan started MP18 and tried to chase after the animal.

Chapter Six

Alice

Alice swam to the exit of the cave. She was shocked to see the light shining in toward her. She wondered who else would be diving the cave, then she remembered the ROV from earlier. This annoyed her. Things were already bad enough. The last thing she needed was some asshole submarine destroying her and her friends' visibility. She shewed the ROV off with her hand. The ROV didn't move. She pointed up then to the ROV then up again. It didn't move. She felt angry.

As she approached the ROV she realized one of the lights was flashing. She hadn't noticed it at first and thought it was strange. Why wouldn't this thing get lost?

Now she was really annoyed. She was about ready to kick the damn thing, then she stopped. The light flashed three times quickly, then three times slow, then three times fast, then it paused, then it repeated. It was an S.O.S.! Did it need help? Alice needed to understand. Maybe something happened on the surface. She swam close and examined the ROV. She saw it was holding on to the wall with one of its claws. She looked at the other. There was a sandwich baggie. She grabbed the bag and the arms claw opened. It looked like it was supposed to be a note. Water had seeped in and only a few words were legible.

"Dangerous, Extreme, Follow."

Alice wasn't sure what to make of it. She pulled out her wet notes and hoped the thing would be able to see. She scribbled quickly and made it short and concise.

Deco X2 30@25' 10@15.'

She hoped the operator understood. The ROV released the wall and nodded up and down. At least that's what she took it to mean. The ROV must have had some idea because it led them straight for the anchor line, then it ascended exactly to twenty-five feet and remained motionless. Everyone else seemed just as surprised.

After switching to pure oxygen, Alice pulled out her wet notes and scribbled another message this time for Danny and Marco.

ROV helping warned about danger.

She scribbled another note after handing the first to Marco. As they finished reading it she handed them the second note.

Eyes open might be another animal.

Alice held up the okay sign with her free hand; her other hand was holding the anchor line. Marco held up the same sign and nodded his head. Danny shrugged and rocked his hand side to side as he made the okay signal; the sign for so-so or yes but not really. It was clear everyone was stressed. Their breathing rates were all very high—something Alice could hear from the sound of their regulators. Everyone wanted to be out of the water. Luckily, nobody was darting for the surface in a panic, which was good.

Alice used the time to look over at the ROV. On closer inspection she noticed the homemade nature of the sub. The overall shape was that of a rectangular box. It had two very large tubes that were obviously PVC pipes at the top. It was boxed in with a cube shaped cage of much smaller PVC. There were parts that were clearly 3D printed. Other parts looked like they had been shaped by the teeth of a rabid dog. Some parts had marks of furious coercion, signs that they had to be forced together. Most of the ROV was a soft white, but some of the smaller parts were lime green.

Various lights blinked within the clear dome where the camera was. It had six propellers. Four spaced like you would see on a regular quad copter drone pointed vertically. Then two more in the middle pointing horizontally in line with the body. It had two arms that ended with claws for grasping. Then it had a yellow cable knotted around the back and plugged into some sort of connector.

After a minute, Alice started to zone out and think about Pat. She wondered what had happened. Where did the thing come from? Was there another entrance to the cave? Could it be out in the river with them? She shook her head at the thought. Danny placed a hand on her shoulder and held up the okay sign. She returned the gesture.

She checked her dive computer...she still had nine minutes left at this depth. As she lowered her arm a sound filled the water. She couldn't see what it was, so she turned around. A dark colored hull was cutting through the water toward the other boat. It was the unmistakable hull of a Marine Patrol vessel. They must have called Marine Patrol. She wondered what happened on the surface that would have made them call the police. Things must be pretty bad if they sent the ROV to warn them and called in the Marine Patrol. Were there more victims? Was someone hurt? Had something happened to their boat?

This line of thinking wasn't doing her any good. She needed to worry about her own problems. They needed to focus on the task at hand. A member of their dive team had been killed. Also, the creature that did it was still in the water and could be nearby.

Alice thought back to the thing she saw in Infinity Deep. She tried to remember what it looked like. Maybe if she knew what it was, she could have better chances against it. Whatever it was, it was massive. It was longer than their boat...so maybe twenty feet? She wondered what could be inside the cave that was that big. She searched her mind for more details. All she saw was a colossal, black mass moving through the water. It was silhouetted by Pat's dive light. How could something so big get inside the cave? There had to be another entrance or a new passage that led to the surface.

Alice wondered if it came from some underwater cavern that had been sealed off until recently. If that thing was living underground for this long, it must have been eating something. What if there were more.

She shivered at the thought.

Alice glanced around and checked her dive computer. It was time to ascend to the next stop. She waved at the ROV and pointed up. She wasn't sure if it noticed. They were probably busy with the police. Alice and the other two divers swam up the anchor line until they were at fifteen feet, then adjusted their BC's to compensate for the change in depth.

The ROV sprung to life and scanned the area around it, then it looked up the anchor line and ascended to Alice and the others. They were only fifteen feet from the surface. They were now in the layer of water filled with tannins. The water was now a deep dark coffee color; the sun above them looked an orangish green. It was difficult to see the water below. Visibility had been reduced from over a hundred feet to only about twenty. They could clearly see their own boat, but anything below them would be almost invisible.

Alice squinted in the direction of the other two boats above the sink hole. She couldn't see anything. It seemed like the ROV noticed the lack of visibility as well. It dropped down a few feet. Just below the tannin layer. Alice could see the ROV pretty well. It was still relatively close, and its lights were very bright. The ROV hovered like a phantom in the water as it whirred. Alice couldn't help but be reminded of the wraith from a movie she watched when she was younger.

In that movie, a woman lay sleeping in bed blissfully unaware of the impending doom hovering above her. The camera paned over her face as the ghastly figure hovered only inches away from her. A chill ran down her spine at the comparison.

Suddenly, the ROV shot off like a bolt of lightning. Alice was shocked at how fast it was. She didn't expect it to be able to move like that. She watched as the light disappeared into the darkness of the tannin stained water. Then the water rumbled. The sound of a tremendous roar echoed through the silence. It felt like the water itself was shaking.

Alice's heart started racing.

She looked at the others. Their eyes looked like they were about to explode out of their masks. Everyone wanted to get out of the water. Almost in unison they checked their dive computers. Alice had to wait the longest, since she went the deepest. She knew right away she would be left alone.

Marco bolted for the surface right away. He probably had long since passed his decompression obligation. It was likely both Marco and Danny were only waiting for Alice's sake. Danny looked back briefly to Alice. Then the creature roared again and he left her.

Alice felt more alone than any other moment in her life. Even more alone than when her sister died. She had never been afraid of open water before now. Now when she looked down, all she could imagine were the long sharp teeth of a gaping, hungry maw lunging up from the darkness below. That's when she noticed her breathing. She needed to calm down. Her decompression tank had nowhere near enough capacity to sustain her current breathing rate. She looked up. The boys were already out of the water. They were safe. They weren't in danger. They were on the surface.

Alice was staring death in the eyes. Hell, she wasn't just face to face with death. She was down right shoving her tongue down death's throat. She was a measly fifteen feet from the surface. Fifteen feet might as well have been a mile. If she bolted for the surface, her fate was certain. If she stayed in the water and finished decompressing, she would at least be in control of the situation.

She looked at her dive computer again. She grabbed what she could of her composure and squeezed it like a vise. She got her breathing under control, and assessed her situation. She had seven minutes left. Dive computers always erred on the side of caution meaning she likely wouldn't have to wait quite as long. She was breathing pure oxygen which sped things up as well. She had over-breathed her rebreather at least once though. She over exerted herself a lot. That would make her decompression take longer.

Alice imagined dive tables in her mind. Numbers, graphs, charts, all flashed in her thoughts. She was stressed but she was still confident in her math and understanding of dive tables.

Five minutes.

Five minutes and she would slowly ascend. Alice didn't like cutting things this close. Decompression sickness was serious and potentially fatal. She doubted she would die from such a small discrepancy, however, getting out of the water didn't guarantee her safety. They still needed to get off of the water too. She needed to be at her best. She needed to get out of the water soon though. There was no telling just how much danger she was in at the moment.

Alice focused on her breathing and tried to calm down. She reverted back to an exercise she had learned in therapy.

She imagined a place in her mind—somewhere perfect. Somewhere safe. She imagined a temple, and she walked inside. The temple was made of black glossy stone. The walls arched up to a crystal domed ceiling. The walls were carved with stunning and beautiful reliefs depicting scenes of unimaginable beauty. One was of an ocean scene, where a noble marlin leapt from the waves chasing flying fish. One relief was of a majestic moose drinking from a mountain stream. Another depicted an eagle plucking a trout from an alpine lake.

At the top of the room, the light filtered in through a glittering crystalline rotunda in a rain bow of color. The beautiful color was shifting and swirling on the floor.

Four minutes left.

The columns holding up the ceiling were each meticulously carved with elaborate scenes as well. One was carved with a scene of a girl in a long flowing dress chasing butterflies in a wonderful garden. One of the other columns was carved with a glorious still life of a marsh surrounded by strong, towering cypress trees. Elegant cranes flew above the marsh. The next column pictured a fantastical reef with all kinds of fascinating fish. Each one was bathed in the transcendent light from the ceiling painting it with a natural brush of breathtaking splendor. The floor was lined with the softest grass she had ever stepped foot on. It caressed her feet as she walked to the last column. The final column depicted the night sky. Stars twinkled and glimmered in the light.

Three minutes.

In the middle of the temple was an island surrounded by an impossible, babbling stream with no beginning or end. Giant koi the size of station wagons swam blissfully around the island. The koi were splotched with a chromatic sheen that seemed to reach beyond what the human eye could comprehend. A small bridge made of floating logs led to the island's center.

Alice stepped on the bridge in her mind's eye and she could feel the cold water splash up on her feet. The logs were worn perfectly smooth by the flow of the water. The island was lined with stone pedestals that made a privacy curtain of flowing fern like vines that draped down from their pots as far as they reached up toward the crystalline rotunda. A small fountain greeted her on the island. The water flowed over its bowl into a small basin beneath it. Its purpose was obvious to her. She stepped forward and washed her hands and feet. She had to wash the outer world away before stepping foot on such precious ground.

Two minutes.

This place in her mind was the most sacred thing she could conceive. The safe place she retreated to when the world was overwhelming. Once she was here, she was safe. Nothing else mattered but that moment.

The island was carpeted with more of the infinitely soft grass. In the center was a tree. It weeped like a willow. The leaves were spaced far apart and shaped like tear drops. The leaves glistened with sap that seemed to glow in the paltry light that cascaded from the veiled sun that was so very far away. At the base of the tree, the ground reached up in the shape of a cradling chair. She laid back into the earthen chair now connected even more to the earth than she already was. The grassy throne was perfectly shaped, it contoured exactly to every curve of her body.

One minute.

She looked up and watched as water fell in a torrent from the mouths of statues that lined the edge of where the domed roof met the crystal. Each statue resembled a noble creature. A lion, an eagle, a stag, an elephant, a humped back whale, and a wolf. They all spilled their roaring bounty into the small body of water that encircled the island. It roared loudly with the sound of a raging waterfall. It was deafening and soothing at the same time.

Then she started to ascend—slowly, patiently.

She looked down, but nothing was there. Then she looked behind her. The light of the ROV was blindingly bright. Then suddenly, the ROV was reduced to rubble and scrap before her eyes. The monstrous beast grabbed it in its jaws and bit down as it rushed past her. It passed by so close that the current from its wake almost ripped her off of the anchor line. The monster thrashed and spun in a whirlpool of rapid white flushed water.

Alice swam up and before she could even reach for the boat Marco and Danny were ripping her from the water. The force of the sudden jolt pulled the regular from her mouth. She gasped for air and collapsed into Marco and Danny as they pulled her away from the edge of the boat.

They fell into a heap of bodies. Alice ripped her mask off then she looked for Danny. She pulled her fist back and punched him as hard as she could in the face. She coughed as she ripped her gear off and tried to catch her breath. Danny held his nose and screamed.

"What the fuck!? We were trying to help you!"

"F-huh...FUCK YOU! YOU FUCKING...h-huh...LEFT ME! YOU ABANDONED ME!" Alice screamed at the top of her lungs as she gasped for air.

Alice flung her bail out tank to the side trying to hit Danny with it. Marco stepped back not wanting to attract any of Alice's ire. Alice collapsed on the ground and started to sob.

"I watched Pat get eaten, then you fucking abandoned me. What the actual fuck? What the hell is going on? I almost got eaten too! If it wasn't for that fucking sub, I would be dead right now. Marco, don't think you're free and clear either! If it wasn't for the fact that I know you love Patty I would kick you in the fucking balls. But you Danny? Seriously?! After what you told me last night?"

"Oh yeah?! Well when the fuck were you even planning on giving me a chance huh? I've been friend zoned by you for years! Did I ever fucking complain? NO! I was happy just being around you. I told you how I felt. I told you what you meant to me. You just brushed me off. All you ever did was stomp on my heart! What do I even matter to you anyway..."

"Nothing now! To think I was actually considering being more than friends with you. The fact that I was going to give a snake piece of shit like you a goddamn chance! Fuck off!"

Danny stood up and marched over to the helm. He started the engine and lowered the prop into the water. He looked down at Alice as she was trying to compose herself on the floor of the boat.

"Can one one of you get your shit together and pull the anchor so we can get the hell out of this fucking place?" Danny growled.

Marco and Alice looked at each other, then at Danny.

"You know what. Why don't you fucking do it your self," Marco said then spat toward Danny.

Marco started helping Alice to her feet and Danny strutted toward the anchor.

"I guess I'm the only one who wants to stay alive in this hell hole," Danny snorted.

He bent over and tugged the anchor line. The anchor came loose and he pulled it up. When he got to the chain he stopped and looked around nervously. Then he pulled the rest of the anchor out of the water. He coiled up the rope and tossed it toward Marco.

"Can you at least put it away? Thanks," Danny grunted.

Danny walked toward the helm and Alice pushed him aside.

"This is my fucking boat. I'll take the wheel. You can sit in the back. Enjoy the view while you can because it'll be the last time you see my ass," Alice said with venomous disdain.

Danny looked like he was about to say something, but then he thought better of it and took his seat at the back of the boat. He stretched out with his arms wide across the transom of the boat.

Alice put the boat in gear and throttled up the engine. The boat lifted up into motion and then it stalled and didn't move. Alice was about to throw the throttle all the way forward until she heard Danny screaming. The monster had leapt from the water and sank its teeth into the engine. Danny was shrieking in pain. The beast had grabbed one of his arms and pinned it to the transom. It bit down harder and ripped the engine off of the boat. It took most of Danny's arm with it. Danny flailed and screamed as he clutched at the tattered remains of his forearm. Alice rushed over to try and help. Danny kicked at her as he flailed around helplessly.

"Fuck you! Get the fuck away from me you fucking whore!"

Alice looked down at him with contempt. The boat was sinking and Danny was sliding back towards the missing section of the hull. Alice almost hoped the creature would return and do its best impression of *Jaws.* Alice turned and looked the boat over. She needed to do something and she needed to do it quickly. She wondered about the Marine Patrol boat. She wondered if it could help. She worried if it would even be able to. Alice still didn't know why it had been called.

As she thought, Marco tore apart the boat looking through the compartments under the seats and in the hull. He grabbed the dry box and removed the flare gun. He broke the pistol open, stuffed a flare inside, aimed high, and pulled the trigger. He sent the flare up into the air with a long, arching trajectory. Marco jumped from compartment to compartment tossing the contents out frantically. Alice tried to make sense of what he was looking for. Then she realized he was as clueless as she was. He was hoping to find something that likely didn't exist. They needed a hail Mary.

Chapter Seven

Cody

The Marine Patrol boat rumbled toward where the thing had just been. Cody still didn't know where the animal had gone. He descended the ROV back below the Tannin Layer and started looking around. Then he spotted it. It was turning straight for the dive boat. Cody wasn't paying enough attention earlier. Only two divers had left the water. One was still clinging to the anchor rope.

Cody pushed the controls forward. He had to save the diver, even if it meant losing the ROV. As the ROV approached the diver, Cody thought of how peaceful she looked. He gripped the control firmly and in an instant, years of hard work were turned into fragments of shattered dreams. Cody bolted upright and looked over to the dive boat to see if it had worked.

Before he had a chance to look, the boat jolted out from under him. Cody fell flat on his ass. Brian clung to the rail on the gunwale at the bow. Jose collapsed just like Cody. Mark fell overboard. The boat was dragged about twenty feet before the tether for the ROV got caught on the propeller of MP18. The two Marine Patrol officers were tossed like toys from their boat as well. The engine of MB18 cut off and Garcia climbed back aboard and held out his hand for Garagan.

Cody got to his feet and looked around the boat. Then he realized Mark was missing.

"Mark! Where are you buddy?"

"Mark's gone?" Brian asked as worry filled his face.

"Here! I fucking fell in! Jesus get me the fuck out of the water! I fucking told you we should leave"

"What the fuck happened?" Jose asked.

"The thing got tangled in the ROV tether. Toss Mark the life ring!" Cody answered, then shouted at Brian.

The ring flew and landed about four feet from Mark. He paddled towards it and grabbed on. Brian held the rope tied to the ring and pulled hard. The old sunbleached rope snapped.

"Shit!" Everyone yelled in unison.

Mark started kicking towards the boat. Cody heard the dive boat start its engine and looked over. It looked like all three divers were out of the water now. That's when Cody remembered. There were originally four divers. Cody wondered if it was the cave or the creature that had got the fourth diver. He turned his attention back to Mark.

"Mark, come on man! You got this. It's nowhere near here," Brian called out.

"It's probably still picking parts of the ROV from between its teeth," Cody added.

"Shut the fuck up and just get ready to pull me up," Mark chuckled slightly.

All of the men on the boat gathered around the transom and pulled as Mark gained his footing. They grunted as Mark was pulled back aboard the Diligaf. Jose handed Mark a towel and he started to dry off.

They all breathed a collective sigh of relief now that everyone was back on the boat. They looked over to MP18 and it looked like they were back onboard their ship as well. The dive boat throttled up, and they all turned to look as it was about to take off.

"Wow, not even a thank you?" Mark said indignantly.

Then, in one swift and aggressive motion, the beast grabbed the back of the boat trying to flee. This was the first time anyone had gotten a good look at the business end of the animal. Its head was strange; it looked like a cross between a manatee and a gharial. Its jaw jutted out the front of its face and was lined with long, conical teeth that interlocked with each other. It had strong and powerful muscles to the back on either side of its jaw. Its eyes were large and bugged out of its head. They had horizontally slit pupils like a frog. It was deep bodied and its skin was rough and pale grey. The animal thrashed around and ripped part of the boat off with it. They saw someone convulsing around near the damaged hull section.

"We can still move right? The crash didn't fuck our boat up did it?" Mark asked.

"I think so let me check."

Cody turned the engine on and looked over to the Marine Patrol boat. They hadn't moved since the collision with the ROV cable. Cody assumed the cable probably got caught in the propeller. Cody pushed the throttle forward and the boat moved.

"Hey! Get the anchor up. We have power. We need to see if we can help them!"

Mark pulled the rope from the cleat and started pulling up the anchor. Hand over hand of rope piled onto the deck as he leaned over the bow. He tugged the line in as fast as he could, still soaked from being thrown from the boat earlier. The sweat forming on his face was indistinguishable from the water still dripping from his hair. Once he got to the chain he went to heave the anchor straight into the boat.

Pop! Fizzz!

Everyone turned to look at the dive boat. They watched as a bright red flare rocketed into the sky. While everyone including Mark was looking to the sky. The creature sprung from the water as if it was attached to the very chain Mark was pulling. It rested partially on the side of the boat. The monster was aiming directly at Brian as it slid forward. He had nowhere to go; his face was fixed with a look of abject terror.

In one swift motion, Mark swung the anchor over his head and slammed it down into the side of the beast. Flesh was ripped away by the savage blow. The hit was so hard the animal shifted and turned slightly. The beast rolled its weight on the side of the boat and swung its head toward Mark.

Mark leaned back to brace himself, but slipped in surprise. The motion saved his body from the monster's rows of sharp, jagged teeth. Unfortunately, it put its snapping jaw right in line with Mark's head. The beast turned back the other way and tore Mark's head from his shoulders. A stream of blood splashed across the deck of the boat as Mark's headless corpse collapsed. The beast slid off of the boat and back into the water. The anchor fell in Mark's lap, his hands still clenched around the rope and chain.

Cody slammed the throttle forward and the boat sprang to life. He had no idea what he was doing, but he knew he had to do something. He grabbed the air horn and signaled to the dive boat. As he drove the boat to them, Brian placed a towel over Mark's body.

Cody pulled alongside the dive boat. Brian and Jose held out their hands to help the divers aboard the Diligaf. Marco and Alice jumped aboard as Brian hopped on the dive boat and ran over to Danny.

"Leave him! He got what he deserved," Alice yelled.

"We can't just leave him. Somebody give me a hand," Brian called out.

Marco went back and grabbed Danny by the feet. Danny had passed out by the time they had gotten on board. Brian and Marco lifted Danny over the side of the boat where Jose and Cody grabbed him and set him down on the Diligaf. Brian and Marco jumped back on the boat, and Cody turned them around toward MP18.

As Cody steered the boat, Brian and Marco tended to Danny's injured arm. The attack was not clean. Long strips of flesh dangled from the exposed bones of his forearm. Jose grabbed a length of cord from one of the compartments and used a screwdriver to tighten the makeshift tourniquet. As he did this, Brian had finished dressing and bandaging the stump as best he could.

Jose almost had the tourniquet fully tightened as Danny sprang awake. He screamed in pain and flailed around. Brian and Marco held him down. Danny's eyes went wide then rolled back and he passed out again.

"What the fuck was that?" Marco asked.

"Tourniquets hurt like hell. It was probably the pain. He's probably going to remain unconscious for a while," Brian responded confidently.

Cody pulled the Diligaf alongside of MP18 and shut the engine off. Garcia tossed over a line and Jose tied off the front. Garagan tossed over a second line and Cody tied it off near the stern.

"Are you okay? What happened to you guys?" Cody asked.

"I'm not sure. We hit something in the water. It got tangled in our propeller. We are sitting ducks now. What about you? Are you guys okay?" Garcia replied.

"The boat is still okay. We have one dead, one hurt really bad. One of the divers is missing," Cody explained.

Garcia radioed the information in. Then he started storing his rifle. Alice looked up, surprised that Cody had noticed Pat was missing. She looked over at the dive boat that was now sinking. The bow was pointing toward the sky as it slowly receded into the murky water.

"What are we waiting for?" Alice asked bluntly.

"She's right we need to get out of here," Cody agreed.

"Not so fast, son. We shouldn't act without thinking." Garcia paused. He looked and fixed his gaze on the dive boat.

"What do you mean? We need to get off of the water. As long as we're on the water we're in danger...unless you know something we don't?"

"Well let's think about it for a second. When Miss Valentine was with her friends, when did the monster attack?" Garcia asked.

"I'm not sure I remember."

"When did the monster attack the dive boat? Do you remember what happened right before the attack?" Garcia inquired further.

Everyone thought deeply for a moment.

Garcia continued, "I think this thing is attracted to or angered by sound. It seems like it's most aggressively attacking when there is a loud noise."

"Why don't we test it?" Brian suggested.

"How do you plan on doing that?" Wendy asked.

"We can put the bluetooth speaker in one of the dry bags, toss it out and blast some engine noise or something," Brian suggested.

"What have we got to lose? If we can distract this thing long enough, we might be able to at least get to dry land. All we have to do is get to shore," Jose reasoned.

Jose made it sound so easy. Brian stood up quietly. Everyone looked around at the water's surface. The river was still, almost calm. Brian turned on the speaker and connected his phone. He lowered the volume and searched for the right video to play. Brian tossed the speaker into the dry bag and closed it up with plenty of air so it would still float, then he chucked it as far as he could from the boat. It landed about seventy five feet away. Then he played a video of a loud, roaring engine.

As he turned up the volume the water around it began to tremble from the bass and sound. Just as they had suspected, the animal broke the surface and snatched the speaker in its teeth. The bag popped and the sound disappeared with the monster.

"It worked!" Brian shouted.

"So, now what? What does this do for us?" Alice asked incredulously.

"Now, we distract it and make a run for it," Cody explained.

"Okay, but how? What's the plan?" Jose asked.

"Our boat is useless, but it's also built like a tank. It would be very hard for the animal to sink or destroy it completely. I say we turn it on and tie a rope to the throttle. Once we are far enough away, we set it to full throttle and wait for the show. Then we gun it. Take off down river to the dock," Garcia explained.

"I like it, but, well...who is going to be on the boat to turn the engine on. How are they going to get off? Also, how are we going to get away from the boat quietly? Are you willing to try and see if a paddle is going to piss this thing off? Sorry to be a Debbie Downer but, there are holes in the plan," Alice reasoned.

"No, she's got a point. We need to figure out a solution to those problems. Is anyone good at throwing a lasso? We could try and throw a rope around one of the cypress knees near shore," Brian pointed out.

"I'm pretty good. I've had to lasso a few runaway PWC's in the past," Garcia answered.

"Well that's one problem solved. Who is going to turn the engine on? Not to mention how do they get off safely?" Alice replied.

"I'll do it," Garagan answered.

"Okay, cool. Thanks for your sacrifice," Alice responded sarcastically.

"Yeah, we need a way to get you off safely," Brian concluded.

"I'll just turn it on and jump into this boat as Garcia pulls the boat to shore," Garagan answered.

"I don't know if I like that. What if you fall in? What if your jump is loud enough to cause the thing to attack? It doesn't sound like a good idea," Brian explained.

"Okay, what if I lean across, and as soon as it starts, Garcia pulls us away from it? Wouldn't that work?" Garagan asked.

Everyone paused in thought for a moment. No one really liked the idea of being close to the boat while the engine was turned on. No one had any better ideas.

Brian spoke up again, "Okay, so here's the plan: Garcia ropes the shore, we tie a line to the throttle, Garagan starts the boat, then we pull ourselves to shore. Did I miss anything?"

"No, I think that covers it," Alice answered.

Everyone nodded in agreement.

Garagan leaned over and tied a small cord to the throttle. While she did that, Garcia tied one end of the lasso to the boat's starboard bow cleat. He tied a slip knot on the lasso side and stood on the bow. Garagan leaned over the port stern side and gripped the key. Everyone was ready. Garcia twirled the lasso over his head, narrowed his eyes, and let the rope fly. The lasso landed right on the bank in a mess of cypress knees. The middle of the rope splashed in the water gently. Garcia pulled the rope taught.

"Okay, now Garagan!"

Garagan turned the key in the ignition slightly. Then the entire boat jolted toward shore. Garagan turned to yell at Garcia to slow down. Garcia screamed in pain as the boat was pulled out from under Garagan. As subtle as it had been, the splash of the rope was enough to anger the beast. It snatched the rope and tried to rip it away from Garcia. Garcia had wrapped the rope around his arm and was trying to hold on with all of his might.

The monster leapt from the water and jerked its head from side to side. The sudden shock caused the rope to rip into the meat of Garcia's arm. As the rope pulled free it tore through his flesh. Once the rope was free from his hand, he turned away clutching at his mangled arm. The rope coiled at his feet began to fly out into the water. Then one of the coils looped around Garcia's foot. The rope went tight again and ripped Garcia off of his feet and pitched him overboard. His head cracked against the gunwale on his way out of the boat.

Everyone's attention was on Garcia and getting him help. His unconscious body was dragged into the water. His life vest kept him on his back as he was dragged across the surface. Jose jumped into the water and swam for Garcia. Everyone was screaming.

"What are you doing!"

"Are you crazy!?"

"Jose! Be careful! Don't splash around!"

"That dude is fucking nuts," Marco uttered under his breath.

Jose swam for Garcia to try and get him back to the boat. No one realized that Garagan had fallen over the stern. Everyone was paying attention to Garcia when he was dragged over.

Garagan was terrified.

Her head bobbed under the water first and when her life vest pulled her up, the motion forced water up her nose. She choked and coughed as she tried to get her bearings. The water stung her eyes as she blinked. The water in her lungs kept her from being able to call for help. She continued to hack and struggle for air.

Meanwhile, the rest of the group was chanting and encouraging Jose. They threw water bottles, shoes, and anything they could get their hands on to try and distract the thing. Wendy stopped for a moment. She just barely made out the sounds of Garagan struggling in the water over the commotion.

Wendy turned toward the sounds of Garagan's struggle. She saw her coughing and struggling to get out of the water and jumped into action. Wendy tried to pull Garagan up, but in Garagan's panic she pulled Wendy down. She almost fell in the water. Luckily, she caught herself. She leaned forward with both hands and pulled Garagan with all her might. It was no use. Garagan was in such a panic that Wendy couldn't do anything but hold onto her. Garagan's panicked thrashing was making a lot of noise. Too much noise. Wendy called out for help when she realized Garagan was too much for her on her own.

"Help me! Garagan's in the water too!"

Alice and Marco were the closest. They both turned around. Cody turned his head and Brian was still locked in on Jose and Garcia. As Alice realized what she was looking at her blood ran cold. Marco had a similar reaction, his eyes grew wide as he looked on realizing the danger. Unlike Jose and Garcia who were making very little noise and splashing as little as possible. Garagan was flailing wildly. It was the perfect picture of what not to do.

Wendy screamed for her to calm down and stay still. Garagan couldn't breath though. Not only was she terrified of the animal she was sharing the water with, she was drowning. Her lungs were filled with water. Her body was screaming for air that she couldn't get. Her mind was panic stricken and demanding she be out of the water. She had no control over her movements. She was in a frenzy.

Alice took a step toward Wendy. Marco tried to get around the bench behind the center console. Then they felt it. Something had brushed against the hull. It was almost gentle—the sensation of the creature sliding along the boat's bottom. The boat wasn't the thing's target though. If the boat was its goal, it could have knocked all of its occupants into the water. The boat wasn't what it wanted. Garagan's frantic thrashing figure was the sole object of its desire.

The beast's power and fury were immense. It erupted from the water violently. So violently in fact, that it didn't just grab Garagan. Alice reached forward and grabbed Wendy's ankle. She tugged as hard as she could to get her away from the edge. She pulled, hoping and praying to get Wendy away from the villainous explosion of violence.

From Marco's vantage point he saw everything in traumatic detail. It played out in slow motion before their eyes. Garagan was eviscerated instantly. Wendy almost pulled Alice over the edge of the boat as the beast went by. Alice collapsed to the ground as Wendy's body slumped back into the boat. Everything above her navel was gone. Her entrails dangled down from the boat's gunwale. Blood spilled from her disembodied pelvis.

On the opposite side of the boat, things were not any better. Jose had made it to Garcia. Jose had to focus on his own issues. He had no idea what had just happened to Wendy and Garagan. Jose grabbed Garcia by the life vest and gently doggy paddled to the boat.

As Jose swam, he felt something in the water with him. It was the rope! Jose took a deep breath filling his lungs with air to help him float. He pulled Garcia close to using his life vest as well.

"Cody! I've got the rope! Pull me in!"

Cody scanned the edge of the boat frantically until his eyes found the rope. Cody pulled the rope and the line went taught. It was still anchored to the shore. The rope could not be pulled in.

"Jose! It's still tied to shore! You'll have to pull yourself in. Just go slow! Try not to splash around."

"Easy for you to say!"

"We have to do something!" Brian shouted.

As Brian turned to look for anything that could help, but when he saw what was left of Wendy, he knew something had happened. He had no idea it was that abominable though. He froze for a moment—partially from the trauma of what was in front of him, and partially because he had no idea what he was even looking for.

Brian clenched his eyes shut. He thought about the situation. He pictured in his mind what was happening and what had already happened. Then he remembered.

Garcia had a rifle. He had shot at the creature earlier. Now where was it? It had to still be on MP18. They drifted away from the boat when the monster grabbed the rope though. He wondered if the smaller line attached to the throttle was still on the boat. Brian's eyes sprang open and groped around the boat.

"That's it! It's still here," he called out.

Brian lunged for the small cord and started pulling. Cody felt the strain in his arms as MP18 was being tugged closer.

"What the hell are you doing!?"

Brian realized his mistake and stopped.

"Sorry, I was trying to get back to the patrol boat. Garcia's rifle is still on it I think."

"What good is an AR-15 going to be against a fucking whale?!"

"It's better than nothing! What else are we going to do?"

"Fine, Just don't pull so damn hard. You nearly pulled my shoulder out of its socket."

Brian started pulling again, this time slower and more gentle. Slowly but surely the MP18 started to inch closer. As this was happening, Alice pushed aside Wendy's mutilated corpse and tossed the first thing she could find over it. She didn't want to see what was left of the poor girl. Alice didn't know who Wendy was but she knew she deserved much better than this. She died trying to save someone. If Alice got out of here alive, she would tell the world of the brave sacrifices that were made today. Alice looked at Marco. She placed her hand on his shoulder.

"We need to keep our heads on straight. If we are going to make it out of this alive we need to be in the moment. Are you with me?"

"Yeah, I'm with you, Alice."

"Good, grab whatever you can and start throwing it as far away as you can. We need a distraction if those two are going to have any chance at survival."

Alice and Marco grabbed anything they could find and chucked it as far as they could. It seemed to be working. The fin of the creature swirled around the objects they threw and even snapped its jaw at some of them.

As Marko searched for more things to throw, he saw Danny still had sandals on his feet. He grabbed the shoes and Danny stirred. Marco glanced at Danny briefly to make sure he wasn't seeing things. He tossed the first sandal, then looked down at Danny. Danny's head was shaking. Marco chucked the other shoe. Then he looked back again. His eyes were starting to flutter. Danny was regaining consciousness. Marco wasn't sure if this would be good or bad. He nudged Alice.

"Be careful, Danny is waking up. Who knows how he'll react. He could be violent."

Marco pointed this out to Cody as well. Soon, the mood on the boat shifted again. It was like they were being attacked from all sides at once. Cody was worried about what might happen next. Tensions were rising. Jose was only a few feet from the boat. Cody would need help getting Garcia out of the water. Cody looked behind him. MP18 was not very far off either. Soon, it would be close enough for Brian to get on board and search for the rifle.

Cody thought about Danny. He wondered if he would be dangerous. Having a gun on board seemed like it would be a bad idea somehow. Cody wasn't sure what was about to happen, but something felt wrong. He felt as if whatever happened next would decide whether or not anyone would survive this ordeal.

"Guys, I'm going to need help getting Garcia out of the water. Get ready to give me a hand. Brian, when you get on the patrol boat stay there. I don't want that gun on board until we know what we are dealing with as far as Danny is concerned. Do you all understand?"

"Me and Marco will help you with Jose and Garcia," Alice confirmed.

"And once I have the gun I will stay on the boat until Danny is calm, or passes out again," Brian answered.

"Alright, let's do this."

Chapter Eight
Cody

It's hard to describe the feeling that Cody was experiencing at that moment. He had gotten everyone here. Not just physically, but through his actions. It was his idea to take the ROV to Buffalo Breakdown. They could have taken it anywhere else. Most of the group wanted to take it out on the Gulf. Cody had insisted the visibility would be better and the water would be calmer on the river. It was his decision to help the divers. It was his action that destroyed the ROV, and disabled the Marine Patrol boat. Cody had made a lot of decisions that made things worse and got people killed.

At the end of the day, he was the reason they were all in this situation. The realization crashed over Cody like a tidal wave. His heart ached, his stomach twisted itself into knots, and his mind screamed at him for answers he didn't have. Cody shook himself out of it. Those things didn't matter right now. The past was behind him. All of his past. What mattered was doing everything in his power to save everyone he could. And right now, Jose and Garcia needed him.

Jose had been Cody's first new friend when he moved to Florida. They bonded over their love of fishing and wildlife. Jose was a good man. He loved and respected nature more than anyone else he knew. He didn't deserve to die, especially not like this.

Once Jose was close enough, Cody reached down and grabbed his arm. Jose squeezed back. Alice and Marco grabbed Garcia. In a swift and decisive motion, they all pulled the two out of the water. Jose jumped up on his feet as soon as he was on board. He threw his fist in the air and cheered triumphantly. He and Garcia had survived the encounter.

Meanwhile, Brian had gotten MP18 close enough to climb aboard. As the rest of the group splashed and pulled the men from the water, he was searching for the rifle. As brian spotted the rifle, he heard a commotion on the Diligaf. Brian grabbed the rifle and brought it to his shoulder; he kept the muzzle at a low ready as he surveyed the scene before him. Danny was awake now. He had gotten to his feet and began screaming. He searched each person in the group's face with eyes made of accusatory rage. For whatever reason he focused on Jose. It was likely because he was the closest person to him that he did not recognize. He hurled incoherent accusations at Jose with bigoted fury.

"WHAT DID YOU DO TO MY ARM!!! I WANT IT BACK! GIVE IT TO ME YOU FUCKING WET-BACK, SPIC, PIECE OF SHIT!"

Jose was not about to take such abuse, even if it was from a delusional person with a grievous injury. Jose swung on Danny and his head snapped backward from the hit. To everyone's shock he didn't get knocked out. Danny stumbled slightly and turned back toward Jose with furious hatred painted across his face. He went to swing his stump at Jose but Marco grabbed him from behind. Danny swung around and pummeled Marco with his good hand. The pair tumbled onto the deck as the fight raged on. Jose kicked Danny off of Marco and Danny flailed back to the stern of the boat. Cody wanted to help, but he and Alice needed to tend to Garcia. Besides with Brian it was three against one, one armed man. It was only a matter of time before they had him subdued.

Marco stood between Jose and Danny. Danny was writhing on the ground. When he stood up they realized he wasn't writhing on the ground, he was struggling trying to get his dive knife free with only one hand. Danny held the knife over his head and lunged toward Marco. Brian raised the rifle, aimed and pulled the trigger.

Click.

Brian's heart sank instantly. The worst possible sound imaginable was a click when you were expecting a bang. There wasn't a round in the chamber. Brian turned the safety off, checked the magazine, but never made sure a round was chambered.

Brian and Jose watched in terror as the knife disappeared into Marco's neck. Brian grabbed the charging handle and chambered a round as the glistening red blade unsheathed itself from Marco's neck. Marco slumped and toppled over into the water. After the splash, there was a rumbling snarl as his body was snatched by the monster. By the time Marco's body was eaten, Brian was locked in and aiming at Danny. Jose yelled.

"Stop! Don't fucking do it!"

Bang!

The rifles report sliced through the air and echoed across the water. One round was all it took. The interior of Danny's skull was now exterior. His body collapsed in place as if someone walked up behind him and hit his off switch. Brian was the one that said they couldn't just leave Danny behind. Now he was the one who had killed him. If he hadn't said anything, Marco would still be alive. Now two men were dead.

Brian released the breath that he had forgotten he was holding. The rifle almost fell from his hands as he began to relax. He was still in shock over what had just happened. During one single breath two men had died. He wondered what he had just done. What had he just witnessed? What was he supposed to do now?

Alice grabbed Garcia's arm. It was bloody and the skin was burnt and torn, but it wasn't life threatening. He would likely make a full recovery. She bandaged it and looked over his head. He had a big goose egg on the back. It didn't look too bad, but brain damage is rarely visible, unless it's really bad.

Brian stepped back onto the Diligaf, a changed man. He stepped over to Danny's body. He looked at what remained of his fatal decision, then he looked at the towel covering Mark's body and at what remained of Wendy.

Brian looked out over the river, took his vape out of his pocket, and prepared to take a drag from it. He stopped. He looked at the device—really looked at it. He drank the image in as thoughts passed through his mind. Then he looked at the spot where Marco's blood had pooled; it was still wet. His eyes narrowed and he chucked the vape into the water. It splashed and started to hiss like a malevolent serpent as it sank into the darkness.

"I hope you fucking choke on it," Brian said to the creature.

"What do we do now?" Jose asked.

“I don’t know...maybe we can try shooting at the thing?” Cody supposed.

“We could still try and distract the thing. Then we could shoot at it while it's distracted. Maybe we will get lucky and kill the thing, or we can scare it off?” Brian suggested.

“How do we plan on distracting the thing? The plan with the patrol boat doesn’t sound very appealing any-more after last time,” Alice said, expressing her reservations.

“What about this? Hear me out. What if we leave the Diligaf?” Brian recommended.

“Wait, are you fucking telling me this boat is named the Diligaf? You have to be fucking shitting me. Wow...sorry, you were saying we should abandon the only functioning boat? Do go on," Alice said while rolling her eyes.

“Look, this boat is filled with corpses—that’s undeniable. I know I don’t want to stay here. I doubt all of you do either. We still have the rope tied to shore. We bring that over to the patrol boat. We start up the Diligaf and send it off down the river. Worst case scenario the monster bites the engine off immediately, best case it follows it far away and leaves us alone.

If it attacks the boat right here I’ll pump it full of lead. If not, we are basically home free. Garcia said that the patrol boat was basically unsinkable. ‘Built like a tank.’ If we were marooned on a boat, I, for one, would rather be on the one built like a tank. What do you guys think?”

No one really wanted to respond. The plan sucked. It was the best they really had to go on though. Everyone looked at Alice.

"What are you staring at me for? I don't have a better idea. It sucks, but it makes sense. We will need to move Garcia to the patrol boat though."

"Okay, let's do it," Cody agreed.

They picked up Garcia and moved him over. They set him down on the bow of the boat. Cody stayed on the Diligaf. He looked the boat over. This boat had been his redemption. It was the muse that pushed him forward. It hurt him deeply to send it off in such a way. As he tied the steering wheel in place a tear ran down his cheek. Before the boat, he was alone. Since he started with the ROV project, he felt like he had actually made progress in his life. He knew it wasn't the boat that did these things, but the boat was there for all of those moments.

Cody looked around. Not only was he leaving the boat, he was sending away the corpses of people he knew. People who woke up this very morning, blissfully unaware of their impending demise. His hand was shaking as he placed it on the ignition. He didn't want to leave them. He couldn't just abandon them. He never wanted to turn his back on another person ever again. Yet here he was...about to do it again. How was this any different? He didn't come to Florida to run away from his problems, he had come here to face them. To overcome them. He wouldn't walk away from these people. He would send them off.

Cody dragged their bodies to the bow. Then he doused them in gasoline and grabbed the flare gun. A Viking funeral was still a funeral. It was how Cody would want to go out if he could.

"Okay, I'm ready! Throw something!"

Jose chucked a water bottle far away in the direction the Diligaf was facing. Cody waited a second. When he saw the water start to swirl, he fired the engines. The boat quietly rumbled alive. Cody hopped onto the gunwale, leaned over and put the boat in gear. Alice and Jose grabbed him as he forced the throttle forward and the boat lurched. He would've fallen in if his friends weren't there to catch him. Cody stood fast and fired the flare. Brian stood poised and ready with the rifle. He was ready to blast the animal as soon as he saw it.

The boat burst into flames. The motor whined as the boat picked up speed. Then, just as they expected, the boat was attacked. The creature sprang forth and bit down on the port side. Brian unleashed hell into it. The monster roared, this time above the water. The noise was much higher pitched above the water. It sounded like a deeper version of a dolphin's chirping laugh. The animal thrashed and dove back into the water. Everyone was happy to see a large pool of blood where the thing was.

Brian had hit it and appeared to have done a lot of damage. When the monster grabbed the boat, it changed the boat's trajectory. Instead of heading up stream away from the patrol boat, now it had turned. The boat had taken on some water from the attack as well. The combination was beginning to look deadly. The boat hadn't been facing back at first, but the listing hull had caused it to start turning more.

The Diligaf was now fully aflame and on a collision course with MP18.

Jose dove for the rope connected to shore. Everyone started tugging at it. Every inch they pulled seemed to pull them further into the path of the runaway boat. Cody watched in horror as the boat bared down on them, and his mind couldn't help but return to that fateful night years ago.

Cody would never admit it, but he knew why his wife had left him. The event was set in motion by the worst decision of his life. Cody and his friend Glen were out drinking. It was a Friday. With no work in the morning they got hammered that night. When they went to leave Glen insisted he was too drunk to drive home. Cody had been a little more conservative than Glen that night, not by choice, but simply because he couldn't afford more alcohol.

In a moment of foolish arrogance, Cody asked Glen for the keys to his truck. Glen handed them over gladly. He didn't pause even for a moment. It was simply something they were accustomed to doing. Besides, Cody was almost sober, sure his vision was a little blurry but he still had his balance and his wits about him. As they thundered along Cody looked down at his phone to text his wife. He knew she'd be pissed if he didn't let her know what was going on. He started typing the message.

> ***Cody:*** *Hey baby, im with G. Gunna stay at his plce tnite...had to drive him home srry.*

Before he could hit send he felt a bump and looked up. He was heading straight for a massive boulder. He tugged the steering wheel, but the more he tried to steer away, the more the truck turned toward the massive rock. What he didn't realize was that the truck was skidding on the dirt. He needed to turn into the slide, not out of it. He was doing the exact opposite of what would have saved them. It was as if they were in slow motion as the rock barreled towards them.

Then, the truck slammed into it.

Cody strained as he was slammed into the seatbelt. The airbag filled the truck with a terrible burning smell. He remembered it as feeling almost soft against his face. He coughed and fumbled with the seat belt trying to get out of the truck. Cody stepped out without a scratch. The seat-belt and airbag had done their jobs perfectly. Glen was not wearing a seatbelt. He was ejected about forty feet from the accident. Cody stood shocked and disgusted. Glen was crumpled against a different large rock. His body was compressed and twisted into a shape not meant for a human being. The bloody heap that was his friend twitched and groaned in an almost squeaky cry.

Cody ran back to the truck. He searched for his phone, but when he found it, the screen was shattered, the unsent message to his wife was still there waiting. Cody deleted the message. He closed the door to the truck. He looked over to where Glen's body lay. There was nothing left that he could do. Nothing would bring Glen back. It was far too late for that. He decided he would leave Glen behind and walk home. They lived in a small town. People would realise he hadn't come home and they would look for Glen and find him. At least that's what Cody believed would happen. They would find the crash site, conclude he was driving and got ejected. There was nothing to suggest Cody had ever been there.

That's not what happened though.

The police wouldn't be called for three days. Glen's body would be scavenged and would rot in the hot Arizona sun. By the time his body was found, there wasn't much left to connect Cody to the truck. The cops knew Glen wasn't driving though. They would interrogate Cody multiple times. During the last interrogation the detective said it flat out.

"I know it was you. You're a piece of shit for leaving your so-called friend to rot like that. You saw the pictures. His eyes and tongue were ripped out. His mother had to identify his body. I was there. She cried her eyes out for that boy. I fucking hope you get what's coming to you. We are closing the case. I can't prove it in court, but I fucking know it was you. I hope you rot in hell."

The strain of the investigation took a lot out of Cody. However, it was the guilt that ruined him. Cody was drunk and scared when he made the initial decision. He wished every day since he had done things differently. He wasn't the same man after that. The weight of Glen's death was immense. He was sober every day after that night. He never turned himself in or confessed. Cody had always felt the guilt of that choice. To this day he still felt as if there was a cosmic debt that remained unpaid.

Once again, Cody was looking on in horror as impending doom barreled toward him—death's cloak exchanged for a cape of flames. What he had once viewed as his salvation was now set to destroy him. If they hadn't tried to pull themselves out of the way in the first place they might have made it. If they had pulled a little harder. If they just got a few more handfuls of rope in. That wasn't what happened though.

The Diligaf collided with MP18 at full speed. The Diligaf's hull splintered, flames erupted into a towering inferno, and the inflatable portion of the patrol boat was torn and deflated. Jose was leaning over the gunwale when it hit. He was crushed and ripped off of the boat. Alice was thrown backward and Brian dove on to the deck. Cody was thrown from the boat by the impact. He was alerted to the outcome when his body was embraced by the frigid water of the river. He was looking up at the rays of sunlight trickling through the water. Only it wasn't sunlight. It was the roaring blaze of the Diligaf.

He swam upward, and as his head broke the surface, he looked around. The burning heat of the conflagration bathed his face like a sunburn. The Diligaf was sinking in spite of its engine trying to push it up out of the water. The flames persisted on top of the water even as the boat sank. As the outboard motor was fully submerged, the engine flooded and died. The only remaining sound was of the blazing firestorm and water rushing up onto the patrol boat. With the inflatable portion popped it was sinking lower in the water. It wouldn't sink completely, but it would take on a lot of water.

Cody wasn't far from MP18, so he started swimming. As Cody splashed about everyone on the boat collected themselves. Alice looked around and assessed the scene before her. Brian was still getting up. Garcia had shifted and was now laying in the water that was starting to fill the boat. Jose was gone, and so was Cody.

Cody pushed past some debris in the water and was about to climb aboard, when the object he was using for leverage was soft and squishy, he made the horrifying realization that it was Jose. Cody flashed back to visions of Glen. The way Jose was crushed left his skull similarly deformed. His upper half was smashed and battered.

Cody pushed away and frantically tried to put distance between him and Jose's mangled corpse. As he did Brian and Alice realized where he was. Alice leaned over and grabbed Cody. As he splashed around, the monster returned.

Alice screamed as she saw the large spiny fin rise up out of the water illuminated by the flames behind Cody. Brian grabbed the rifle and aimed at the beast. Alice was starting to lift Cody out of the water as Brian took aim to blast the animal with another volley of bullets.

As he fired, the creature turned its ire to Brian. Brian emptied the rest of the bullets in the magazine into the fowl thing. It was not enough to stop it though. It rose up and snatched Brian off of his feet. With a despicable crunch, Brian was torn asunder. Alice and Cody were left alone with Garcia, surrounded by a wall of flames. The flaming fluid swirled atop the water and was inching ever closer. Time was running out.

Chapter Nine

Cody

The boat was sinking. Alice and Cody had no idea if it would sink completely or not. Garcia said the boat was very difficult to sink, but not impossible. Right now the boat was taking on water and shifting to one side. Alice lifted Garcia's head, trying to keep it above water, and looked around, scrambling for any kind of plan to get out of the current situation.

Cody limped to the bow where Alice and Garcia were. The cold water was coming up to their knees as the sweltering heat wrapped around the rest of them. The water rose over Garcia's chest and he started to stir.

"Officer Garcia? Are you awake?" Alice asked.

He groaned in reply. He wasn't entirely awake but he wasn't unconscious either. It was obvious his injuries were severe. He was hurt badly, and he would be no help in whatever happened next.

The boat seemed to have stopped taking on water. It was floating with about two feet of water on board. The flames however, had not stopped. They were still creeping in closer. Cody looked around, there had to be something to help. The rope tied to shore was floating about fifteen feet from the boat. They were drifting slowly down the river, inching further from the rope, and closer to the flames. Something had to be done. There was no telling if the monster was still around or even alive.

As the thought entered his mind that Brian might have killed it, a loud splash erupted behind him causing the fire to swirl around. It was still there. The only direct line to shore and safe dry land was getting further and further away. There might have been a better option, but the option in front of Cody would work. The time to think was over. The time for action had arrived and it was now or never. Cody plunged back into the water. Alice gasped in surprise.

"What the hell are you doing?!"

Cody couldn't hear her over the splashing of the water around him. He was focused and resolute. As he swam, the rope came closer. He thought of how he had abandoned Glen. He thought of Mark's sacrifice, Marco's murder, and Jose's Brave attempt to save everyone. Brian gave his life so that Cody could live. Everyone Cody considered a close friend was gone. Their lives wouldn't be lost in vain. Cody was going to survive and he was going to save Alice, and Garcia.

Cody grabbed the rope and turned around. He was fifteen feet from the boat. It seemed like it was an impossible distance away. It was a mirror image of how Cody had saved Alice.

Alice reached down and grabbed her dive knife. She looked down and found the boat hook. She grabbed what she could and fixed her dive knife to the boat hook, making a makeshift spear. She stood poised over the gap between Cody and the boat ready to strike.

Cody paddled as quietly as he could, trying not to splash. In return, his pace was very slow. Then the rope started to go tight. He was approaching the end of it. He still had just over an arms length to go.

Alice turned the boat hook to Cody, pointing the spear end away from the water. Cody grabbed the boat hook and pulled. The boat came closer. Cody grabbed the side of the boat and looped the rope on the cleat. Then, just like clock work the monster came for Cody. The beast crashed through the water slicing through the paradoxical inferno with ravenous hunger.

Cody tried to clamber aboard but he couldn't gain purchase and slipped back into the water. Cody placed his feet against the hull and prepared to spring himself off of the boat. It was dangerous and bold but there was nothing else he could do with such little time.

Alice flipped the spear and raised it high overhead. She took in a deep breath and screamed with righteous fury as she drove the spear into the animal's thick hide. The behemoth roared and thrashed, turning away from Cody as he sprang away from it. It swirled amongst the blaze draping itself in the fiery fluid. The sudden movement pulled Alice into the water with the foul creature as it spun and thrashed.

Alice wrapped her legs around the thing as best she could to gain leverage. Flames whooshed and danced around her as she drove the spear back down. She shoved the spear deeper into its flesh. When she did, the monster shrieked an ear-splitting howl of pain. It's started to thrash slower. It flexed and convulsed as the water turned deep red with the blood spilling from its new wound. What fuel remained on the surface began to burn off as the blaze began to recede.

Finally...it was over. The dangerous beast was dead. Cody swam over to Alice to make sure she was okay. The animal slumped and floated on the surface as the fire licked its hide. The smell of burning flesh began to fill the air.

"Are you okay?"

"Fuck yeah! Holy fucking shit! It's dead! It's really dead! We fucking killed it! HRRRAAA!!!"

Alice screamed in celebration and let out a primal roar of victory. They swam to the shore and pulled in the patrol boat.

As the boat brushed against the shore, Cody grabbed Garcia and carried him on to the riverbank. As Alice and Cody tended to Garcia, the sound of a helicopter chopped its way into their ears. Soon, they saw the helicopter flying over the sinkhole. The paltry amount of flames that were left were extinguished by the down draft. The helicopter scanned the shore and they waved at it. The helicopter lingered and examined the remains of the giant creature. Then a voice came over the loudspeaker.

"Stay where you are! Help is on the way! Stay out of the water! There may be more."

Alice and Cody looked at each other wearily at the thought of more of these things. Then they collapsed on the dry earth taking in a deep sigh of relief. Cody looked over to Alice.

"Where did you get that rebreather?"

"I built it. I couldn't find one that did what I wanted, and shaped the way I needed it."

"That's so fucking badass. Not as badass as riding on the back of a sea monster and spearing it to death in a maelstrom of flames. Still pretty badass though."

"Thanks. Who built that sub?"

"I designed it. Brian made some of the parts. I built it. It cost me a lot. I don't know if I'll be able to make a new one."

"That's pretty cool too dude. You'll build another one."

"Thank you for saving me."

"You saved me first. I was just returning the favor," Alice replied.

"Still I appreciate it."

"Don't mention it."

"How long do you think?" Cody asked.

"Till what?"

"Until the government death squad shows up and kills us to cover everything up?"

"Ha! You're funny. I don't know, fifteen twenty minutes?" Alice chuckled.

"You think hit squads have snacks? I don't want to die on an empty stomach."

"If they do it's probably crap. Like vegetarian jerky, or freeze dried deviled eggs."

"That sounds disgusting. I really hope you just made those up."

Cody and Alice talked nonstop the entire time they waited for the emergency responders to arrive. The first to arrive was the trauma helicopter. Garcia was airlifted to the nearest hospital. The paramedics arrived next and after they cleared them both medically. The police began their investigation.

Cody and Alice didn't bother with hiding the truth. The mountain of death and destruction that lay in the wake of what unfolded was all the credibility they needed. It was very clear that something horrible had happened. As they explained the events and how they unfolded, the interviewers looked on in disbelief. They were certain something incredible was responsible for the devastation. What Alice and Cody had described was far from what they were ready and willing to believe though. The cops didn't think that they were being deceitful; they just couldn't be brought to believe such a fantastical explanation.

Before they parted ways, Cody and Alice exchanged numbers to keep in touch.

When Cody got home that night, there was a car he didn't recognize in the driveway. It was an extremely nice German sports sedan. It looked as expensive as it was fast. As Cody walked up the driveway the door opened. A man stepped out and met Cody half way. He was dressed neatly in a polo shirt and dark colored jeans. He had no facial hair and wore a friendly, welcoming smile. He seemed a little younger than Cody. He would have thought he was a salesman if not for the late hour. As he introduced himself he held out his hand for Cody to shake.

"Evening boss. Sorry to bug you at your home, but time is precious. Have a seat."

Chapter Ten
Cody

Cody was very confused. If he wasn't afraid of the potential consequences he would have told the individual to fuck right off. Despite the man's calm demeanor Cody got the sense he could be very scary if he so chose. When he took his seat in the front of the sedan he was surprised to see a woman in the back seat. She was even more casually dressed. Her hair was up in a loose ponytail. She wore an oversized hooded sweatshirt with a graphic on the front Cody couldn't make out due to its clumsily folded posture over her midsection. She sat cross legged with a computer resting on her lap. She clacked away at the keys as he settled in.

Cody was pleased to find his seat was not just comfortable it was heated and already warm. The environment was very disarming.

“Alright, Mr. Reynolds, is it okay if I call you Cody?”

Cody wasn’t exactly surprised, but it did catch him off guard that they knew his name. He supposed they probably knew lots of things.

“Sure, I guess. What’s this about? Who are you? Am I in trouble?”

“Cody, we are going to record this conversation. Is that okay? It has nothing to do with any kind of trouble. You are not in trouble at all,” the woman in the back said, still typing on her computer.

“I don’t mind, but I want to know who you are and what this is about.”

“My name is Tony, this is Maddie. We work for the Organization that oversees incidents like the one you experienced earlier today. We need information so we can resolve any safety concerns. We would also potentially deal with the people responsible for what happened. If that applies,” Tony stated.

Cody nodded.

“Okay, let’s start off easy. You ready,Cody? Can you tell us about the creature?”

“It was big. Like twenty feet, maybe even thirty. At least twenty feet long though. It had a tall, spined dorsal fin.”

“Do you remember how many spines it had?

"I'm not sure. Maybe ten?"

"Okay, go on."

"Umm, it was wide, like wider than a horse. It was a very pale grey. It had weird eyes too. Like frog eyes. It had a long snout lined with massive teeth like a gar fish. Way bigger teeth proportionally though."

"Okay, what else can you tell us about it? Weaknesses, behaviour, ways we can find it. Things like that."

"It roared like nothing I have ever heard. Remember that movie with the giant preying mantis that came out last year? Imagine that but deeper and like, I don't know. Clicky? Raspy? It was weird. Very loud too. It was extremely attracted to sound. It seemed like sound really pissed the thing off. It was deep inside one of the caves too. Now that I think of it I don't think it had a blow hole. I didn't hear it breathing at all I don't think."

"How did you kill it?" Tony asked.

"I'm not really sure. We don't know if there was more than one or if it was the same one the whole time. If we were only dealing with one? Well, let's see. We rammed it with an ROV, smashed it with an anchor, shot an entire mag of .223 into it, and we stabbed it with a spear while it was on fire."

"Holy shit. I hope for everyone's sake there was only one," Maddie exclaimed.

"Did it have any identifiable markings? Like paint, colorful tags or bands, maybe a piece of metal with a number on it?"

"I can't really say I was looking for one, but no, I didn't see any."

"Did you happen to see what direction it came from?"

"No."

"Did you notice any strange smells or feelings around it? Did anything like really weird happen, I mean like crazy weird? The kind of weird you'd remember instantly," Tony continued.

"No."

"Okay, That's all we really needed Cody. Thank you very much. I'm sure you are very tired."

"Wait, hold on a second...I have questions. Where are you guys from? What are you going to do? Can you help me out at all? Are you able to pay for my boat?"

Tony and Maddie turned toward each other and shared a smirk.

"Mr. Reynolds. We work for The Organization, a company that oversees these kinds of events. We are going to continue to investigate. We are going to make sure the general public is safe. We are also going to make sure any and all responsible parties are dealt with. As far as compensation, what did you have in mind?"

“Well my boat was destroyed. My ROV is gone. All of my friends are dead. I don’t want to have any issues with the law either.”

“You want to deal with this?” Maddie asked.

Tony nodded and Maddie stepped out of the car and closed the door. Cody tensed up worried about what ‘dealing with this’ could mean. Tony shifted in his seat so he was directly facing Cody.

“Here’s what I can do. I can very easily make sure you don’t have any legal trouble. I could give you money right now, but it wouldn’t be much. That’s not how we operate at The Organization. File a claim through your insurance company. I will make sure you are taken care of. We will take it from there.”

“So that’s it?”

“Yep, you’re free to go.”

“Do you have a card or anything?”

“I do.”

Tony reached into his shirt pocket and pulled out a single, plain white business card. Cody wondered if he hadn’t asked if he would have given him the card. He wondered if it was just another form of misdirection as well.

Cody exited the car and waved goodbye to Maddie. She smiled politely and took the front passenger seat Cody had just left. The car's engine growled aggressively, then Tony put it in gear and pulled out of the driveway. The rumbling engine purred as the car drove away. Cody walked in the door and was greeted by his frantic and worried aunt. She ran over and hugged him.

"I was so worried about you when you weren't home on time. Where is the boat? Who were those people?"

"It's a long story I'll tell you over some reheated stroganoff. The boat is gone. There was an animal attack. I have no clue who those people were. They gave me a card but I have a feeling that isn't going to explain anything," Cody sighed, exhausted from everything.

Epilogue

Cody

"Thirty four people reported dead, seventeen people reported missing at Hom-puks-chee-hatchee state park. Still there are no new developments. Florida fish and wildlife have reported that an escaped saltwater crocodile is responsible for the attacks."

"I don't think we have ever seen such a large animal attack in the state's history. I really can't express enough that this was a one off incident. The animal in question has been contained. We are currently investigating where the animal came from. The party responsible will be brought to justice. They will be prosecuted to the fullest extent of the law."

"Assistant Executive Director Cutler said this in a press conference late Sunday evening, 'The families of the deceased are demanding swift action from state officials. Of the seventeen people still missing, twelve were students of Fleming University. The students were celebrating another successful win against their rival DCMU. Many of them were attending the river party on kayaks, canoes, and other small non-motorized craft. Among the deceased was local Mayor Douglas Rothberger's son Theodore. Mayor Rothberger refused to comment on the topic.' In other ne-"

"C'mon Eddy, turn that shit off. That's the last thing we want to hear about," Cody grunted.

"Sorry, I just want to know if anything new came out. How are you doing? Where's Alice?"

"She's coming. She had to work late at her other job. I'm still trying to deal with insurance. They keep wanting to inspect the boat. I keep telling them it's evidence at the impound lot. I still don't have access to it. They are trying to say it was fraud because the boat was deliberately set on fire."

"Shit? Really? That fucking sucks man. You'll get your money back though. They have to give it to you."

"I hope so. It's not looking good though. Those fuckers from the government are still nowhere to be found. They said they would take care of it and I haven't heard shit."

"I still think that's crazy that you got harassed by the *Men in Black*," Eddy told him.

"Not exactly what I would call them. They were definitely not wearing suits."

"Yeah but, creepy dudes from the government. Asking you all kinds of questions. Telling you they will clean up the mess. What organization did they say they were from again?"

"That's the thing, They just kept saying *'The Organization,'* like that was supposed to mean something. The card they gave me said the Department of Agriculture Division of Enforcement and Licensing. It just had their name on it though. I tried to call the local branch and ask for his name. The only thing we could find was the Department of Agriculture Consumer Services. They have no idea who these people were."

"Yeah, dude. That's some straight up *Men in Black* type shit. Do you think they know where the thing came from?"

"I have a feeling if they didn't they were going to find out."

"Where do you think it came from?"

"I don't know, Eddy. We had those earth quakes, and there's all that shit that has been going on with DeSanto, Oscar, and Mandrill. Triple M is all wrapped up in it too. I'm more worried about if there are more of those things."

"Do you think there are more of them?"

"I have no idea. What I do know is that Hom-puks-chee-hatchee State Park is still closed. The fact that the thing took the abuse it did makes me wonder if we weren't fighting more than one. That girl, Wendy, was attacked much further upriver than where we were. After hearing about what Alice found in the cave too, I just don't know. I wouldn't be surprised if there were more, but there just isn't any concrete evidence for it."

"I'm sorry I keep bringing it up, man. It's just fucking wild that you were there. That you saw what you did. I can't believe Alice jumped on top of it and stabbed it to death."

"Not quite how it happened, but yeah. Believe me, I understand. I would be asking as many if not more questions if I were you. I just wish I knew more than I do."

"It's quiet in here now. It feels weird without them here," Eddy said solemnly.

"I know what you mean. I keep looking up when I hear the door chime hoping I'm going to see Brian. Everytime I hear a motorcycle I'm expecting to see Mark walk in," Cody said as he stared at the door.

"Are you ever going to build another ROV?"

"I will. I worked too hard to give up on it. It's going to be a lot harder without Brian though. This time around I'll actually know what I'm doing."

"What ever happened to the cop you guys saved? Have you heard anything about him?"

"Garcia? Yeah! I forgot! I was supposed to hear how his surgery went today hang on. Let me check my e-mail."

Cody pulled out his phone and scrolled through his inbox. It was nestled between a promotional email from Schroders supermarket and a spam e-mail. Here is what it read.

Dear Mr. Reynolds,

Thank you for your concern about my husband. We are very happy to tell you he has made it out of surgery. They removed the damaged skull fragments and installed a titanium plate. The CT scan showed that the swelling of his brain has gone down. I am very happy to say he is awake and responsive. He is still recovering and will have a lot of physical therapy ahead of him though. He is able to read and write but is unable to talk yet.

The doctors are not sure if he will make a full recovery. They did say the worst is over though. M r.Reynolds, I just want to tell you how thankful me and my daughter are that you brought him back to us. The doctors can say whatever they want, but when I look in his eyes. I know he is back. Thank you for everything. I do not know if you told Miss Alice yet, but he wrote a message to both of you.

He's still very groggy from the surgery, but wanted to thank you. He was told of what you did. We are very sorry to hear about your friends. You have our deepest condolences. Even with everything that had happened, and in spite of the danger you were in,

you still prioritized his safety and survival. We are forever in your debt. If there is anything me and my family can do, simply say the word. You two are real heroes. Thank you both.

If it is okay, I would like to invite both of you to dinner when my husband is back home. I would like to thank you personally for your bravery. I am very happy that you have reached out to check up on us.

We wish you the very best,

The Garcia Family

"What? No way! That's so awesome dude. He made it! You're a hero too! I told you there would be some good coming your way," Eddy jeered.

"I'm just happy there wasn't another death from this thing. The fact that he's going to be okay is just icing on the cake."

"That's fair. I'm happy, that's good news man."

"Yeah I'm happy too. Alice will be ecstatic. I can't wait to show her."

Afterword

Thank you for reading Murder Manatee. I hope you enjoyed reading it as much as I enjoyed writing it. If it's not too much trouble, I would love to hear what you thought of my book. I really don't care about publicity or analytics. I just want to be the best author I can be. Any and all feedback you provide will help me achieve that goal.

I would like to address a few things that happened throughout this story that you might have missed. This story is largely inspired by the White River Monster of Arkansas. Most of the locations are fictional just for ease of writing. One of the first things I did was come up with the name of the river where the story takes place. In the unlikely event that you understand Muscogee (Creek) you would have caught the first of many Easter eggs in the story. The name or more accurately phrase "Hom-puks-chee" can be interpreted to mean: *time to eat, or come and eat.* I thought this was a fun wink to what would happen in the story.

The monster in this story does have a specific origin. You will learn more about this in the third story in the Over Time series. It will also be loosely connected in the next volume of Benthos. I based a lot of, but not all, of these characters on people I know in real-life. They are only loosely based however. Their names have been changed and certain characteristics were changed to better fit the story. To those who inspired the characters I hope you enjoyed your depictions. I meant no disrespect and it was all in good fun.

The opening scene where Cody grabbed the soldering iron actually happened to me one day while I was working on my car. As I mentioned in the preface, I have a small ROV of my own. What I did not mention is that me and my friends built a modular remote controlled camera deployment vessel. This remote controlled boat with a camera and other deployable equipment is what inspired me to write about the home built ROV. My little toy boat is nothing compared to sophisticated research equipment, however, it works and it was a lot of fun to build.

One of the other Easter eggs in the story was Cody's favorite meal being stroganoff. This is actually one of my favorite meals. I wanted something very comforting and homey. Stroganoff fit the bill perfectly. The last subtle nod is the addition of Tony and Maddie. They will be important later.

The general response from Benthos Volume One was far better than I could have hoped for. I am excited for the next entry in the series. It has been a long time coming. I have been working on it since October of 2025. I started this story so you wouldn't have to wait too long for the next entry in the Benthos series. What started as a quick story to fill a publishing gap has become my new favorite entry in the series. I believe Tursas Romuttaa will be even better. I put more research into that story than any of my other books to date. The next book to come out will be Darkness Falls. This is a fast paced sci-fi fantasy that will hopefully knock your socks off. Darkness Falls is a passion project of mine. It was the first story I ever started writing. I am very excited to put it in your hands. Please enjoy this excerpt from Darkness Falls.

Acknowledgements

A special thank you to everyone who contributed to this book. To author E. N. Chanting, thank you for your support and advice. To author Rob Neto, your books, recommendations, and technical advice helped out immensely. I would also like to give a special thanks to my wonderful editor, Abby Woodland. You are the best at what you do. You are not just quick and skilled; your insight is invaluable. To my friend, Will Duray, thanks for spending countless hours talking about developing my ROV and for the digital printing of the supporting parts. "Bula!" Finally, thank you to all the fine and lovely people I interviewed in my research. The stories herein would be at an unimaginable deficit without your wealth of knowledge and insights. I am in your debt.

Darkness Falls

Chapter 3 SAMPLE

Everyone was exhausted from the ordeal. The only goal in sight was to get away to safety. Jahandro took the ship into a section of empty trees hidden in a shadow where no one would spot them. The group gathered around in the rec room of the ship. Seibon seemed agitated.

"What was that?" Seibon asked.

"I told you we were being chased."

"No, Jahandro. You said Bulgoin slave traders were following you, not whatever those things were."

"Well...at the time that's all the knowledge we had. I told you why they were after us. It would be fair to assume they might send something scarier than Bulgoin's."

"No matter what, this changes things. I can't just get you any permit for that section of space. I was planning on just sneaking you past security. If you have this much heat on you, you're going to need more help than the Fairymen are able to offer."

"Seibon, come on. There has to be something you can do. Don't you have connections to the commander of one of those star fleets?" Jahndro asked.

"Yes I do, but that doesn't help if you are being chased. They *might* turn a blind eye to an almost passable forged passport. I could sneak you past security. I *can't* get them to turn a blind eye to a full-on battle. Besides, I'm going to have to call in a favor or two just to get back home without suspicion. I'm already being investigated for my own side projects, let alone yours too."

"I understand that. Deliniaé where was it that your contact wanted to meet up at?" Jahandro asked.

"It's a place called *The Spire.* Does that sound right?"

"It does, it's a big place though. Was there anything else? Anything more specific?"

"No, but I can ask him if he has any better directions."

The ship sputtered back to life and began to jet through the forest. Jahandro wove back and forth through the trees until Tink smacked him on the back of the head.

"Quit screwing around! Get above the trees and fly straight. Enough hot dogging. No one is impressed."

Jahandro relented and flew above the clouds. Deliniaé chuckled and Tink offered a wink in acknowledgement. The ship got to the edge of the large forest and a tall black needle reached up from the ground and tore a gash in the clouds above it. Water sprayed out of the tip from a glorious fountain. The spire looked like the ultimate evil lair.

As the ship grew closer, more details came into view. The spire was lined with spiraling archways to the tip. Each archway contained a series of small stone villas. Some of the arches had shops. Others had parks filled with people playing games and taking in the splendid view of the flowing water trickling down the middle of the path leading up the spire. Jahandro brought the ship to rest in what looked like one of the larger shopping centers.

"Any word from your guy yet, Deliniaé?"

"No not yet. It's not unusual for him to take a while to respond though."

"In the meantime, why don't we check out the area? It looks pretty cool," Vinichay suggested.

"Fair enough. Me and Seibon are going to work on the ship and try to brainstorm a way on to the Nightmare. Tink, I don't care where you go. Just keep an eye on Thomas."

"Ugh whatever. Thomas, come on! We have stuff to see!"

"I guess that just leaves us. Anything you want to do?" Deliniaé asked.

"Not really. I kinda just want to walk around and explore."

The group split up while still being careful not to wander off too far. The street was bustling but not crowded.

The subtle din of conversations, footsteps, and the distant thrum of The Spire was pleasant. Vinichay found his feet carrying toward the park they passed on their way in. Deliniaé followed close behind. As his head began to clear, a question arose.

"Deliniaé, why did we stop talking? I know we didn't want the same things at the time, but I thought we had a lot of fun."

"We had some fun, yes. You had most of it though. I guess you don't really remember how much I had to clean up after you. I had fun too, but you were always running off...chasing adventure. I had responsibilities. I couldn't just keep chasing after you."

"I guess I have always been one to wander off."

Deliniaé chuckled, "That's an understatement."

"I never really meant for that to happen. I should've been more considerate."

"Vinichay, you were very considerate. Still are. We were just going in different directions at different times is all. Why did you set up shop in the City of Dave?"

"I thought it was a good place—strong economy, good security. It was the right place to open a store front."

"How can someone so bold still be so timid? City of Dave is the last place I would expect you to end up. It's so plain, and simple. Come on, you moved there because of me didn't you?"

"It was taken into consideration."

"So, why didn't you call, or stop by?"

"The same reason you didn't, I guess. It's not that I didn't want to, I just didn't make time. I was nervous too."

"You should have—it would've been way better than how you eventually showed up."

Vinichay and Deliniaé crossed the street and walked over the small bridge passing across the little stream. They walked into the park, and took in the scenery. The park was shaped like a large number eight with the stream separating the top and bottom. Black scalloped columns reached up and held the ceiling in a sporadic and uneven pattern. Each column ended in a large, sculpted hand.

At the top of the eight, in the middle loop, was a small pond. The bottom of the eight hung over the edge of The Spire, held up by massive, black, rough-cut square chains. It provided a large clear view of the edge of the forest. Mist from the fountain atop of the spire flowed down creating a sparkling rainbow just over the edge. The view was beautiful.

"What are you planning on doing after we help Thomas? It's not like we can just go back to normal with Andrew gone and Markus sewing chaos," Deliniaé asked.

"I'll probably move somewhere rural. My clients don't mind traveling. Besides, business would probably be booming right now if I were back home. What about you? Your business isn't as...robust as mine. At least as far as the current political climate is concerned."

"Well as long as my invention takes off, I can sell it from anywhere. I want to travel to the different off worlds."

"That sounds nice, would yo-" Deliniaé was cut off when someone grabbed both of them by the shoulder.

"I don't have much time, and you don't either. I'm with the Enlightened. Deliniaé, the person you are planning on meeting is not your friend. He is trying to hurt you. We can help. I have to go. You should too!"

The figure ran away before they could ask any questions. Not wasting any time, the pair ran as fast as they could toward the ship. They saw Tink and Thomas arguing in front of some sort of bar.

"Come on...five minutes! That's it! It won't take long."

"I told you absolutely not! You are supposed to protect me from danger. How are you supposed to do that while you are inebriated?"

"Guys! We need to go, now! Someone from the Enlightened told me that we are in danger. My contact is not good. He's a rat or something."

"Wait what-what? What do you mean?"

"I can't explain right now. We need to leave quickly!"

The group was back together. Now, they just needed to get back to the ship. Everyone ran, their heads darting back and forth. The warning had paid off. They saw the same group from before, but this time, the group hadn't seen them. They had the element of surprise, but they were between them and the ship. They ducked in an alley and discussed what to do.

“I have a plan,” Vinichay exclaimed.

“What are you thinking?” Tink asked.

“The way you and Thomas were arguing earlier. Do that again. You can take them on from the front. We will need to surprise them. Deliniaé and I will hit them from behind when they’re confused. You smash them and attack them while they’re distracted. Sound good?”

“Sounds good to me. I had a few choice things to tell Thomas before you showed up any way.”

“Good, just remember they don’t know we are here yet.”

Tink shoved Thomas out of the alley, clearly venting some of her earlier frustrations. Then she started yelling at him.

“You are such a prude! How can one man be so damn stuffy!” Tink shouted as she poked Thomas in the chest, almost pushing him over.

The commotion worked. The hooded figures slowly made their way up to the two arguing. Tink perfectly closed the gap, forcing the figures to duck into the alley to try and not be spotted.

Vinichay lunged forward and struck the first figure over the head. Immediately, the figure collapsed. Vinichay went straight for the gun the figure had been carrying. The other figure realized what happened and screamed before Deliniaé could knock them out.

Tink rushed them and made short work of the one Deliniaé was fighting and one more. Five more started across the road, firing hissing lasers in their direction.

Vinichay burst forward from the alley with a volley of laser blasts of his own. The figures ducked, but Vinichay got three of them. Their bodies lay motionless as crowds began to flee leaving the two factions blasting away at each other.

Vinichay looked back. Deliniaé was armed and Tink was stomping on the hand of one of the cloaked figures that wouldn't let go of their weapon.

"We need to move! I'll cover you guys. Get to the ship," Vinichay barked as he provided cover fire.

The group moved behind Vinichay. Tink helped protect Thomas and Deliniaé. Deliniaé cleared the path forward. Vinichay forced his way ahead. This made the figures retreat and regroup on the far side of the road for cover. Vinichay's aggressive tactics were risky but effective. It was obvious the cloaked figures weren't expecting a fight. Only a couple remained, taking pot shots at them.

The group made their way back to the ship as quickly as they could. Seibon and Jahandro had heard the commotion and had the ship prepared for them as they made their way closer.

As the group got onto the landing platform, another group of figures started to arrive. They started firing on the ship too. Jahandro started to take off, causing the ship to hover a few feet above the ground.

Thomas was the first one on the ship. The ship started to get too high to jump on. Thomas and Seibon leaned over the edge. Deliniaé threw down the gun to be able to reach up with both hands. Vinichay and Tink were blasting figures left and right. This gave them enough of a window to get on the ship.

Vinchay threw his gun towards the ship but he missed. Then he jumped. Seibon caught his hand and pulled him up. Tink was next. It took three of them to pull her up. Then, with a rippling crack, the ship was off headed for space.

Tink slapped Vinichay on the back. It was so hard he almost fell over.

"That was amazing, kid! I had no idea you had it in you. You saved all of us. We wouldn't have made it out of there if it wasn't for you."

"What happened? Did you meet with your guy?" Jahandro asked.

"Not exactly. We waited for a while. Then someone from the Enlightened, one I don't know, told us that my contact was bad. Then we ran back toward the ship, and we spotted the group before they spotted us. We were able to jump them and get some of their guns. We got away and we put the hurt on them thanks to Tink and Vinichay. We wouldn't have gotten away if you and Seibon hadn't readied the ship the way that you did."

"So, Deliniaé, what are we doing now? Are we meeting up with the Enlightened?" Jahandro asked.

"I...I don't know. Maybe? They are very skittish. My guy is...let's just say...lower level. I don't have any other contact with them. I know of his superior, but I don't know him personally. I honestly don't even know where to look really. I can send a message, and we can see what happens."

"I know somewhere we can try. I can't promise you an audience with any Enlightened, but I have made deliveries for them there. You can drop me off too. I might be able to come up with a legitimate enough excuse to get a ride from there," Seibon chimed in.

"Okay, what are we waiting for then? Let's go already," Tink said impatiently.

www.ingramcontent.com/pod-product-compliance
Lightning Source LLC
LaVergne TN
LVHW090522110826
845146LV00003B/943

* 9 7 9 8 9 9 8 9 1 0 1 3 5 *